P9-DTO-082

Ambrose Bierce

and the

Trey of Pearls

The Ambrose Bierce Mystery Novels

Ambrose Bierce and the Queen of Spades

Ambrose Bierce and the Death of Kings

Ambrose Bierce and the One-Eyed Jacks

AMBROSE BIERCE

and the

TREY OF PEARLS

Oakley Hall

VIKING

VIKING
Published by the Penguin Group
Penguin Group (USA) Inc., 375 Hudson Street, New York, New York 10014, U.S.A.
Penguin Books Ltd, 80 Strand, London WC2R 0RL, England
Penguin Books Australia Ltd, 250 Camberwell Road, Camberwell,
Victoria 3124, Australia
Penguin Books Canada Ltd, 10 Alcorn Avenue, Toronto, Ontario, Canada M4V 3B2
Penguin Books India (P) Ltd, 11 Community Centre, Panchsheel Park,
New Delhi - 110 017, India
Penguin Books (N.Z.) Ltd, Cnr Rosedale and Airborne Roads,
Albany, Auckland, New Zealand
Penguin Books (South Africa) (Pty) Ltd, 24 Sturdee Avenue,
Rosebank, Johannesburg 2196, South Africa

Penguin Books Ltd, Registered Offices: 80 Strand, London WC2R 0RL, England

First published in 2004 by Viking Penguin, a member of Penguin Group (USA) Inc.

10 9 8 7 6 5 4 3 2 1

PUBLISHER'S NOTE

This is a work of fiction. Names, characters, places, and incidents either are the product of the author's imagination or are used fictitiously, and any resemblance to actual persons, living or dead, business establishments, events, or locales is entirely coincidental.

LIBRARY OF CONGRESS CATALOGING IN PUBLICATION DATA
Hall, Oakley M.
Ambrose Bierce and the trey of pearls / Oakley Hall.
p. cm.
ISBN 0-670-03270-0 (alk. paper)
1. Bierce, Ambrose, 1842–1914?—Fiction. 2. San Francisco (Calif.)—Fiction. 3. Journalists—Fiction. I. Title.
PS3558.A373A85 2004
813'.54—dc21 2003053766

This book is printed on acid free paper ♾

Printed in the United States of America
Set in Granjon with Bandicoot Display

Ambrose Bierce

and the

Trey of Pearls

PROLOGUE

WAR, n. A by-product of the arts of peace. The most menacing political condition is a period of international amity. . . . "In time of peace prepare for war," has a deeper meaning than is commonly discerned. . . . Let us have a little less of "hands across the sea" and a little more of that elemental distrust that is the security of nations. War loves to come like a thief in the night; professions of international amity provide the night.

—The Devil's Dictionary

JANUARY, 1892

In a corner storefront on Jones Street in the Tenderloin, a white-haired little fellow with an unbuttoned vest and a green eyeshade advertized what he called a "Cyclorama" of the Battle of Shiloh. A painted fabric landscape lay on a broad table, hills and dales covered with straggly trees and thick underbrush, Pittsburgh Landing, the Tennessee River, Lick and Snake creeks. Frozen in fierce engagement on hilltops and in canyons were lead soldiers in blue and in gray brandishing bayonets and banners, horsemen with their swords aloft, ranked cannons. This depiction was often viewed by silent men, hats off, hands folded together, moving slowly past this scene of a battle thirty years past through a fume of dust and something slightly rank, maybe glue.

Once I happened by the Cyclorama of the Battle of Shiloh

to discover a single beholder of the scene, Ambrose Bierce seated in a straight chair in the midst of it, a brooding figure observed by the green eyeshaded proprietor from his post by the door. Gas lights sputtered around the room, and Bierce's shadow lay across a hill studded with lead soldiers.

I started to call out to him, but just then he moved a hand as though to change the position of one of the combatants. Instead he let it fall back into his lap. I held my peace and retreated from the doorway.

Ten years ago he had published in *The Wasp* "What I Saw of Shiloh," after which writing about war was changed forever, for he wrote of cowards and deserters crowding along the river bank, fighting not the enemy but their comrades as they tried to board one of the river boats that might take them away from the battle, telling of the brush fires consuming the wounded as they tried to crawl to safety, of a dying sergeant with his brains dripping down his forehead, of the report of a cannon like "a snake striking at the face of a victim," and of the vast relief of Don Carlos Buell's infantry coming to the rescue of Grant's divided and defeated army.

"And this was, O so long ago!" he had written. "How they come back to me—dimly and brokenly—those years of youth when I was soldiering! Again I hear the far warble of blown bugles. . . . I see the tall, blue smoke of camp-fires . . . there steals upon my sense the ghost of an odor from the pines that canopy an ambuscade . . ."

He was the only American writer of any consequence who had served in battle in the War, and in good part because of that he was Bitter Bierce, Almighty God Bierce, "the Wickedest Man in San Francisco," the author of "Prattle" in the *Sunday Examiner* and of this year's *Tales of Soldiers and Civilians.* I had heard him say of his nation that it was created by religious bigots and slave-drivers, and that he would as soon have fought for the Confederacy as for the Union, but I knew that those years of his soldiering were the most precious of his life.

He was a presence so potent in San Francisco that it was said of him that barking dogs fell silent when he paced by them. Young female poets genuflected at the mention of his name. He was, as Gertrude Atherton said of him, the grand panjandrum of San Francisco, and his invectives against corruption, greed, hypocrisy, and what he called "unworth" in "Prattle" were looked upon by many as Holy Writ not because of what he had written, but because he had written them.

He and I were employees of Willie Hearst's *Examiner* at a time when the newspaper was in close combat with the *Chronicle* in the circulation wars. Willie's "stunt journalism," among other things, had elevated crime as well as sports to the front page, and had employed journalists as detectives in murders and mysteries.

SATURDAY, JANUARY 28, 1892

One misty Saturday evening after work Bierce and I trod the portion of the "Saloon Route" between the *Examiner* offices and the Palace Hotel. Blessington's Saloon flung a warm blast of light onto the street. Inside, the free-lunch bar was dominated by an immense Virginia ham cooked in champagne, sharing the honor with a cliff of imported cheese, surrounded by platters of sausages and salami, tiny sardines, smoked salmon, along with gherkins, radishes, green onions, rye bread, pumpernickel, and crackers. Bierce ordered a Sazerac cocktail, I a lager, in the sparkle of gas lights on banks of bottles and back-bar mirrors flanked by gleaming half pillars of polished mahogany, gilt-framed paintings on the walls, white-coated bartenders, and reflections in the broad mirrors of merchants, bankers, judges, and newspapermen such as Ambrose Bierce and Tom Redmond.

Bierce wore a black suit, as he usually did. His hair was graying and curly, as was his formidable moustache. His complexion was so fresh he looked, as someone had said of him, as though he shaved all over. He had a military gait and way of standing, from his years in the War, and he had a slightly clipped British accent, from his years in London. He had always carried a revolver since having been attacked by the husband of an actress he had dispraised in "Prattle."

I was just another young fellow in a brown suit, a stiff collar, and a restrained cravat.

Bierce was confronted by a large gentleman sporting a vast corporation and a handlebar moustache. I knew who he was, the banker William Jaspers, the Noble Grand Humbug of E Clampus Vitas, the great drinkingman's confraternity of the West. Jaspers was often referred to as the Bull Clamper.

"Mr. Bierce!" he said in his Bull Clamper voice. "Glad to meet you here, sir!"

"And you, sir," Bierce said, mutedly.

"The scourge of the feminist movement!" Jaspers trumpeted. "And you, young man?" he said to me, his flat, pale blue eyes regarding me with disinterest.

"Tom Redmond, Mr. Jaspers."

Jaspers turned back to Bierce: "Women have no 'thinker,' as I recall, Mr. Bierce."

Bierce had written that in "Prattle."

"The Clampers are ready for battle, sir! Five hundred of the finest young Christian drinkingmen this side of the wide Missouri sworn that the W.C.T.U. parade shall not march!"

"You refer to the Suffragist Parade as a W.C.T.U. event, do you?" Bierce said.

"That I do, sir! You know as well as I that these temperance females try to conceal their true selves behind the suffrage moniker, Mr. Bierce."

I was pleased to see Bierce in a quandary—opinions similar to his own held by a detestable person. Bierce had a low opinion of women's suffrage, which he said was merely a matter of women voting as their husbands instructed them to, or contrarily voting the opposite of that instruction.

The Bull Clamper stroked his moustache as though to calm it.

"You believe that we hold the same opinions as to female suffrage, sir," Bierce said. "That may be so, but for my part I would maintain that this parade is of no importance and will have no possible effect, while you would muster five hundred Clampers to try to quell it."

"And quell it we will, sir! We will ruffian it! We will dog its tracks, and cross them, and confound them. We will deflect those steel-jawed women, sir. E Clampus Vitas was formed to protect the widder and the orphin, especially the widder, and we will perform our duty!"

"Your duty appears to coincide with that of the liquor and saloon interests," Bierce said.

Blinking, Jaspers swung his big head from right to left like a raccoon considering a bite. "Ah, and it sounds as though yours may coincide with Mrs. George Hearst's announcement that she stands with the Suffragists!"

Bierce absorbed that, unfair as it was. Willie Hearst had never tried to dictate to him what causes to support or attack in "Prattle."

"My cousin is one of the Pearls," I put in.

Jaspers stroked the other prong of his moustache. He had seemed from the onset determined to dislike me, and I had instantly disliked him.

"The trio of Pearls!" he sneered. "The temperance beauties, on the float with Madame Grand Humbug Quinine!"

"*Suffragist* beauties," I said.

"Ha!"

"They will have their protectors," I went on. "Of whom I will be one. To fend off ruffians."

"Five hundred of the finest Christian drinkingmen this side of the wide Missouri!"

"With soft whiskey bellies, I expect."

Jaspers glowered at me. He swung his heavy face toward Bierce with the raccoon-headed mechanical movement.

"And so, Mr. Bierce, may we count on your support?"

"You may not!" Bierce said. "I deplore a battalion of Christian drinkingmen convened to disrupt an event that does not seem to me worth disrupting. Good day, sir."

Jaspers stared at him with an expression that seemed to contain an unwarranted level of hatred. He whispered some rank language and waddled off.

Bierce was finally able to sip his Sazerac. He squinted at me over the brim of his glass. "Your cousin?" he said.

"My father's niece's oldest daughter, Amanda Wilson. She is a Suffragist orator to stir the minds of both genders. She is referred to as the Anna Dickenson of the West. She is a good looker, and a proponent of Free Love. With very high standards."

"One of the Trey of Pearls," Bierce said. "Mrs. Quinan's threesome of beauties dedicated to the cause."

"A very essence of pearldom," I said.

SUNDAY, JANUARY 29, 1892

In "Prattle" Bierce had written: "E Clampus Vitas refers to itself as an historical drinking society. It congealed during the Gold Rush, when Clamper miners would obtain drinking money by making drummers coming through town pay an initiation fee. The society has continued to flourish in modern times. Its motto is *Credo Quia Absurdum,* and members pride themselves on caring for widders and orphins, mainly widders. The chief of each chapter is called the Grand Noble Humbug. For the most part they play sophomoric saloon tricks, although there is some philanthropic pretense. Now they have taken up the cause of anti-suffrage.

"The Noble Grand Humbug of the San Francisco chapter, Mr. William Jaspers, has darkly vowed that his forces of drinkingmen will ruffianize the congregation of earnest females at the Suffrage Parade. He counts his forces as five hundred Christian drinking gents. The ladies will do well to let liquor take its course and watch their steps as they tread among the recumbent and snoring Clampers."

CHAPTER ONE

SUFFRAGE, n. Expression of opinion by means of a ballot. The right of suffrage (which is held to be both a privilege and a duty) means, as commonly interpreted, the right to vote for the man of another man's choice, and is highly prized.... By female suffrage is meant the right of a woman to vote as some man tells her to. It is based on female responsibility, which is somewhat limited. The woman most eager to jump out of her petticoat to assert her rights is first to jump back into it when threatened with a switching for misusing them.

—*The Devil's Dictionary*

TUESDAY, FEBRUARY 7, 1892

The very essence of pearldom, in her complicated and gleaming white dress with its black belt that demonstrated the narrowness of her waist, sat across from me in my rooms with a mischievous expression on her pretty face. She claimed to be twenty-one years old this week, and I had opened a bottle of champagne in her honor.

"Thank you, Cuz," she said when I poured the bubbly into her glass.

"I am honored by the presence of the Anna Dickenson of the West."

She laughed delightedly.

Her announcement of herself as an advocate of Free Love

was on my mind. She was a powerful speaker for the Suffragist cause, and very attractive, with her slim figure, the lock of fair hair falling across her forehead, the speckle of golden freckles on her cheeks, her brown eyes, and her mouth that looked made for kisses.

"The doctrine of Free Love has not made much progress on the West Coast," I said. "Would you inform me how you intend to bring us its blessings?"

"See how you are?" Amanda said, sobering. "You men make a joke of our every effort to achieve equality. Free Love is only an equality, you see, Cuz. Men attend prostitutes, they celebrate ladies of the night, they make every effort to seduce members of the weaker sex. Why should women not have similar advantages?"

"Why, then they would not be the kind of women men love and marry!"

"Yes, Cuz, love and marry and get with child one after another until the poor lady is quite worn out with her pregnancies and becomes a neurasthenic case to be locked away, or—more conveniently—dies; at which time the free-loving man may choose him another bride from the current crop of us."

"I see," I said.

"No, I don't believe you do see, but I hope to *see* that you *see* before I leave this city!"

That sounded delightful. She was in fact in residence in San Francisco for the Suffrage Parade on March 3, after which, with its mentor, Mrs. Quinan of the Women's Suffrage Association, the Trey was off to England to speechify for the Cause. These young female Suffragist orators had been coming to the fore of late.

Amanda perched on a footstool facing me where I sat in my easy chair, champagne glass in hand.

"Bierce and I had a run-in with the Noble Grand Humbug of E Clampus Vitas, who is determined to ruffianize the parade."

She wrinkled her pretty nose. "Oh, those brutes," she said. "They come to my ladies' talks to raise a ruckus. But after awhile they cannot help but listen a little, and a little more, and they quiet down."

"I am sure you are adept at calming the savage breast," I said.

"Well, I am, Cuz!"

"You preach the shocking doctrine of Free Love, as well as suffragism, and they listen?"

"They do."

"But they are looking at you as you speak, and you are very pretty, and very shapely, and they must be wondering if you are available to them because of Free Love."

"Is that what is troubling your mind, Cuz? For you see, I am only available to those to whom I might wish to be available, and my standards are very high!"

"I cannot help but wonder if those standards might include cousins."

"I have nothing against cousins, dear Cuz!" She wrinkled her delightful nose at me again.

"And I do have the intuition that you have not had a great deal of experience exercising your standards."

"I am very new at Free Love. It is only a month or so that I have embraced it."

"Practice makes perfect, as we know."

"Oh, I am not perfect yet!"

"Close to it," I said, with a thickened voice.

She jumped to her feet and came to me. Her brown eyes enlarged as she bent her face close to mine. Her skin was certainly perfect. "That's very nice!" she said. She shaped her lips to kiss me, and the champagne-tasting kiss and its duration did not seem to me to be entirely cousinly.

However, she claimed she must hurry off to meet Mrs. Quinan at the Cyrus Hotel, to plan the speechifying at Pierce Hall this Sunday. There Mrs. Quinan would be introduced by the Reverend Henry Devine of the God Is Love Church on Clay Street. At the meeting Mrs. Q. would speak, followed by another of the Trey of Pearls, Emmiline Prout, followed by Amanda. The third of the Pearls, Gloria Robinson of the birdlike voice, would deliver her bird calls and sing "The Battle Hymn of the Republic."

Amanda did not like it when I made disparaging remarks about the Reverend Devine.

"You must admit his name is redundant, at least," I said.

"He is our good friend!" she said, frowning, and departed.

WEDNESDAY, FEBRUARY 10, 1892

"It seems that our Maker has provided gullible women for the express benefit of the Reverend Devine," Bierce had written in "Prattle," and more besides.

And there was disparagement of the Reverend Devine this morning in Bierce's office at the *Examiner*.

"They say whenever he gives a sermon it is attended by at least fifteen of his mistresses," said Sam Chamberlain, the editor.

"Is he to be criticized because that figure is high, or low?" Gertrude Atherton asked. She was seated on one side of Bierce's desk wearing a tight jacket and a neckerchief clasped with a diamond pin. Her fine head of hair, her fine profile, were somehow always on display. She wrote a column for women on Sundays, "Woman in Her Variety," based on Bierce's "Prattle," but her jibes at the foibles of her fellow women always seemed a little shrill. She was a handsome woman, however, and a great favorite of Willie Hearst's as well as Bierce's. I saw that, like many ladies before her, she couldn't keep her hands off the skull that Bierce kept on his desk, staring outward.

"He has tempered old Calvin to his own uses," Bierce said. "The ladies who are his parishioners cannot bear the thought that a stillborn child is transported to the realms of hell as Calvin dictated. The Reverend Devine pronounces them bound for heaven! All is love and reassurance in his theology."

"Free Love is in the air," I said.

"Ah, Free Love!" Mrs. Atherton said. "I have attended to *that* foolishness this Sunday, you will see."

"Merely foolishness, is it?" Sam Chamberlain asked. He wore a monocle and a gardenia in his lapel. He was a newspaperman from New York, who had worked for the *Herald* there, and in Paris before establishing *Le Matin.* Willie had hired him as managing editor, where his great pleasure was thinking up Gee Whiz stunts for young reporters like me to perform.

"It is foolish because of the Material Necessity," Mrs. Atherton replied. "Women must win their bread by marriage, or by prostitution. Or wealthy admirers. Or rich fathers."

"Victoria Woodhull and Tenny C. Claflin had Commodore Vanderbilt for an admirer," Sam said. "Thus they won considerably more than bread. But I ask if you consider Free Love *merely* foolish, Mrs. Atherton. The fabric of society—"

"Please spare us the fabrics that protect the male and leave the female quite bare, sir!"

"But wifehood and motherhood, Mrs. Atherton!"

Bierce was grinning, finger to his chin. "Wifehood without motherhood, Mrs. Atherton? And vice versa?"

"There are remedies of which every prostitute is aware for foiling nature's demand for multitudes, Mr. Bierce."

"I believe I remember you writing of those remedies, Mrs. Atherton," Sam said. "Which column quite shocked Mr. Hearst, as well as the majority of the proper ladies of San Francisco, considering the volume of mail."

"Does that variety of information shock you gentlemen? You had better become used to that shock, for you will be hearing more of it. Women are beginning to revolt against the multiple motherhood obligations of wifehood. Please mark my words."

"It is shocking to men that women require education on the mysteries of their own physiques," Bierce said.

"They have been kept ignorant by their masters!" Mrs. Atherton flared.

"Calm yourself, my dear Mrs. Atherton."

"I am the calmest of women," Mrs. Atherton said, raising her imperious profile. "These quarrels and queries we are having right here are those the Suffrage League and its peripheral forces wish us to be having. For they demand to change the fabric of society, Mr. Chamberlain, Mr. Bierce, and you also, Mr. Redmond."

"Let the heavens pour out their portents!" Bierce said.

SUNDAY, FEBRUARY 14, 1892

At Amanda's urging I crossed myself and agreed to accompany her to services at the Reverend Devine's God Is Love Church. We took one of the prettily painted cable cars up the Clay Street line.

As a Roman Catholic I had not entered many Protestant churches. It was a not-unpleasant experience with my pretty cousin dressed in blue linen on my arm, her face like a flower encased in a pleated bonnet. The church was a vast low structure, already crowded, though the parishioners were hospitable about making room for us. There was not much ecclesiastical decoration—a simple cross on the far wall and a broad platform jutting into the audience, no doubt the stage for Reverend Devine's performance.

The service was a plain affair, and I emulated my Protestant cousin in the few kneelings and standings called for. Obviously all of this was only preparation for the great preacher's sermon, and I glanced around at the predominantly female audience, wondering about the fifteen or so mistresses he was alleged always to preach to.

With an icewater shock it came to me that my newly Free Love cousin might be one, and I stole a glance at her rapt features as the great man strode out onto his platform. He was an imposing figure, rather portly in his brown, shoe-length gown, with a gleaming face raised to heaven, clean-shaven, and with a high forehead framed by brown curls that flipped from side to side when he moved his head. His voice was so deep it stirred something in me that had no wish to be stirred. Amanda's hand clutched my arm.

"The Gospel of Love!" he intoned, and proceeded to explicate. I was shocked at what I heard from these Protestant lips. For God loved sinners, Jesus loved sinners because they could be saved from their sins! Indeed, sin was essential. Mankind is comprised of sinners, and sinners must sin, Our Lord Jesus Christ will save you *because you have sinned.* It seemed to me he was rationalizing his own sins as a notorious seducer of his parishioners. Amanda was staring at the preacher, entranced. Like the other women of the congregation, she leaned forward to receive his words.

He must have pursued the subject for most of an hour. His

voice was stirring, almost as though it was the voice rather than the words that carried the import. He could mimic men and women; his voice sank and rose in dramatic style. The response of his audience seemed to move him in his turn.

"Sin is the gift of God!" he proclaimed. Amanda was bent forward eagerly to hear the words.

My cousin, if not one of his mistresses, was one of his admirers.

She hugged my arm as we filed out of the church. The Reverend Devine stood by the door in his brown robe, nodding and greeting his flock as they departed. He was certainly a handsome man, with his high forehead, the carefully (I thought) unkempt curls that outlined it, his affectedly shy smile. His eye fixed on Amanda.

"Ah, Miss Wilson!" he called out.

I felt the tension in Amanda's arm. She released herself to curtsy. I was introduced, and shook a limp hand.

"My cousin is a Roman Catholic come to pray with us," Amanda said.

"Welcome, welcome," Devine said. His eyes flicked to not quite meet mine.

"The golden voice of the suffrage," he said, smiling at Amanda.

She curtsied again.

"One day you must come and speak before this congregation," Devine said. "You and I together. We will carry the day. A heartful day!" He showed his teeth in a carnivorous smile.

"The golden voice of reason!" he called after us, as we were forced to move on in the crush of others who desired his attention.

Amanda seemed still in a trance as we walked a bit in silence. Then she flounced a little, and turned her head to smile up at me from within the sheath of her bonnet.

"Did you think it was terrible bosh, Cuz?"

I admitted that I had.

Amanda sighed. "If only he were as beautiful on the inside as the outside!"

I had not thought the Reverend Devine all that beautiful, but it seemed wiser not to enunciate the fact, or to question Amanda's judgment on him. Later I was to wonder if I could have detected the shadow of Cain across his face.

I directed our steps toward Pine Street, for I planned to show my visitor-to-San Francisco cousin the City, in a rig hired from Kelly's Fashion Stables.

....

I was pleased to be holding the reins of a spanking brown mare, in the rented buggy, at my side my pretty cousin, who had a lovely habit of appreciation.

We drove past the fine homes of Rincon Hill and South Park, where the old southern aristocracy of San Francisco had settled, gazing across the Bay at Contra Costa County and the cities there: Oakland, Berkeley, and Alameda. For the first time it seemed to me that Rincon Hill looked a little shabby now that the mining and railroad tycoons had begun building their mansions north of Market Street.

I informed Amanda that the oval of South Park was a copy of London's Berkeley Square, and, when this impressed her, sought to impress her further by enumerating the young San Francisco women who had married into European aristocracy: Ella Huntington, Beth Sperry, Flora Sharon, and the Parrott sisters, whose family's mansion on Rincon Hill I had pointed out.

"Chattel property," Amanda said, smiling.

It was the tycoon fathers of young women like these who had agitated for the Married Woman's Property Act so that their daughters could not be victimized by foreign fortune-hunters.

Amanda sighed and said, "I suppose there is no chance for a young woman of no fortune to win a beautiful British prince."

"For beautiful young women, yes!" I said, and she patted my hand.

She was so patty and nudgy, and, in fact, kissy, that I did not yet take her women's rights fixation seriously enough.

We rolled past Woodward's Gardens, where crowds milled in the street and two brass bands contended with each other for sheer noise, and then north to Market Street, rattling over the cobbles in a thick traffic of wagons, drays, buggies, horse cars, and cable cars, in the shadow of the high buildings on the south side of the City's grand thoroughfare. On the city streets there was a twenty-miles-per-hour speed limit.

I reined the brown mare up Post Street to show Amanda the great French department stores, The City of Paris and The White House. After-church couples crowded the sidewalks, ladies with wasp-waists, immense sleeves, many-gored skirts, and broad-brimmed hats that bore fruits and flowers and staring birds, young blades in frock coats, striped trousers, and hard hats.

"Millionaires and their chattel," Amanda said, and nudged me.

"This is San Francisco," I said. "They may be millionairesses with *their* chattel."

Slipping on the stones, the mare plodded up Nob Hill past Old St. Mary's, my church. On top of the hill we passed the newer mansions of the California gold, Nevada silver, and railroad millionaires looming over the City, with their broad lawns. Represented were the capitalists of the Grass Valley mines, the Southern mines, and the Comstock: the Ophir, Gould & Curry, Yellow Jacket, the Con Virginia; and the railroaders Stanford, Hopkins, and Crocker, whom, with Collis B. Huntington, Bierce called the "Railrogues." Governor Stanford he always printed as £eland $tanford.

Amanda was properly impressed by Hopkins's gothic towers and solid bronze fence that was reputed to have cost $30,000; and properly disapproving of the "spite fence" Charles Crocker had built around his neighbor's house, forty-foot-high wooden walls on three sides of the property the owner had refused to sell to him.

On Van Ness I pointed out the "new" St. Mary's, the cathedral, but Amanda was not much interested in Catholic churches. We rolled along city streets past rows of wooden buildings, scrolled roofs, balconies, bow windows, and arabesque carvings—the City I, a son of Sacramento, loved and cherished.

I swung the mare into the park, where a traffic of carriages spun along the roadways in the January sunlight, along with squadrons of peddling cyclists, the gentlemen wearing knickers, high-necked jerseys, and caps, and the ladies sporting divided skirts, leggings, and tams.

"Look!" Amanda said. "Bloomers!"

We drew up alongside two lady cyclists, who looked self-conscious in their billowing nether garments. I thought Amanda's feminism would be challenged.

"Go it!" she called out approvingly.

When I had returned the buggy to the stables, I hailed a hack for the Central Market, where, in the sawdust-floored oyster hut, I ordered an oyster loaf. We watched Charley

Chong slash the top from a loaf of bread, scoop the loaf hollow, butter the inside, and place it in the oven to toast. Amanda observed the process with wide eyes and her hands clasped beneath her chin. Charley tossed a hatful of the small, coppery-tasting Bay oysters into bubbling butter in a copper pan. When these morsels curled at the edges he salted and peppered them with the solemnity of an acolyte performing a religious rite. He poured the pan of oysters into the buttered loaf, closed down the buttered lid, returned it to the oven briefly, and presented the "squarer" to us on a Chinese plate, along with a chilled bottle of Sauterne.

"Oh, my!" my cousin said, gazing at this feast. "How do we approach this, Cuz?"

I showed her, displaying manly experience and know-how.

We sipped chilled Sauterne and devoured oysters.

"Will you come and hear me speak at Pierce Hall tonight?" Amanda asked me. "I will convince you of the spirit and the truth of Free Love."

I said I needed only a modicum of convincing, if we could have dinner afterward.

CHAPTER TWO

FLOP, v. Suddenly to change one's opinions and go over to another party. The most notable flop on record was that of Saul of Tarsus . . .
—*The Devil's Dictionary*

SUNDAY, FEBRUARY 14, 1892

That night I attended the feminist meeting at Pierce Hall. Mrs. Quinan, called Mme. Quinine by the irreverent, introduced the speakers. She was a tall, sorrowful-faced woman with gray hair in a bun and a harsh speaking voice. She declaimed a poem:

They never fail who gravely plead for right
God's faithful martyrs can not suffer loss
Their blazing faggots sow the world with light
Heaven's Gate swings open on their bloody cross!

Next came the Bird Girl, a slender, big-eyed young woman with a wealth of dark hair, who did bird calls. Some of her audience were clearly Clampers, for they bird-called, rooster-called, and cat-called back, but Miss Robinson persisted, and promised to sing later in the program. The second speaker and Trey was Miss Prout, a dark-eyed beauty who spoke rapidly and matter-of-factly, to set the night's theme.

"The basis of our society is the relation between the sexes," she began. "The principle by which the *male* citizens of these United States assume to rule the *female* citizens is *not* democracy but despotism. Our government is based upon the proposition that all men and women are born free and equal and entitled to certain inalienable rights, among which are life, liberty, and the *pursuit* of happiness. When we women demand social freedom it is simply to demand that the government of this country shall be administered in accordance with the spirit of this proposition. *Nothing more, and nothing less.*

"Those who come to these meetings to howl at us are men who should know that when women get their rights, they will be able to live honestly and no longer be compelled to sell themselves for their bread, inside or outside of marriage."

Miss Prout did not speak long enough to arouse the Clampers in her audience, and I was afraid they were poised to attack Amanda, the last speaker, and the professor of Free Love.

My cousin approached the podium, bright-faced in her sparkling white costume, standing at the podium with her left foot advanced, right to the rear. Her voice was strong, clear, and young, and her little fist pumped up and down as she made her points.

"I stand here before you to call for the abolition of marriage," she said. "It is a terrible curse. It entails more misery, sickness, and premature death than all other causes combined. Sanctioned and defended by church and court, night after night thousands of rapes are committed in the name of marriage. By this accursed license, millions of suffering wives are compelled to minister to the lechery of bullying husbands when every instinct of body and sentiment of soul revolt in loathing and fear. There was never a servitude in the world like the one of marriage!"

She paused here to smile at her audience, where now some restive men whispered loudly among themselves, answered by shushes from the women. Amanda looked disappointed that she had not caused more of a fuss. She proceeded, brandishing her fist.

"I warn the gentlemen here that the woman of the present is not the woman of the past, that one day she will mete to you as you mete to her!"

Here there were some cries of protest from the men in the audience—mostly comical, I thought. Amanda faced them, smiling.

"Marriage is in no way an equal partnership intended for the equal advantage and happiness of both parties. I tell you that there is vile sexual commerce where the dominant power of one sex over the other compels submission against all the instincts of love. Where hate or disgust is present, whether in the gilded palaces of Nob Hill or the lowest purlieus of the cowyards, *there* is prostitution, and all the laws that a hundred state assemblies pass, or a thousand preachers preach from their pulpits, cannot make it otherwise!"

Again Amanda's smile and raised hand quelled cries of outrage. I realized that she gloried in the power of her voice and the ameliorating power of her presence, and I relaxed for the first time, no longer fearful that I was going to have to rise from my seat and beat the stuffing out of some Clamper who tried to assault her at the podium.

So she continued: "Sexual freedom means the abolition of

prostitution both in and out of marriage. It means emancipation of woman from sexual slavery. It means coming into the ownership of her own body. It means the end of her financial dependence upon man. It means the end of forced pregnancy. It means the birth of love children only."

The term "love children" created another outcry, but she faced it down, taking two steps to the right, two to the left, skirts swishing around her ankles.

"There are members of my gender who consider sexual desire vulgar. Vulgar! The instinct that creates immortal souls, vulgar? Who dares stand up amid nature, all multitudinous and beautiful, where every pulse pounds with the creative urge, and utter such sacrilege? Vulgar, rather, the mind that can conceive such blasphemy! I say raise the women's instinct to match the males' and follow God's blessing to perfect the beautiful promise of our full natures!

"Let me tell you a story," she continued. "A woman I feel I know, a good wife and mother. Six children, five miscarriages, her health and perhaps her reason destroyed. Her husband rid himself of her as infirm in mind, into a hospital and away from his house. She died—dead at forty-three! And he is free to marry again, and be the ruination of still another good woman! What a life of miseries that poor woman's was! I tell you, I swear to you, such a life will never be mine!"

And she raised her fist and actually shook it at the men in the audience.

They cheered her to the echo.

At the end the Bird Girl sang "The Battle Hymn of the Republic" in a thin, clear voice, and that was the end of the evening. I took Amanda in a hack to the Poodle Dog for dinner. I could dream of its sinful third floor, but I settled with her in an only partially private booth on the second floor.

Champagne arrived. I complimented Amanda on her orations.

"I'm good, am I not, Cousin?"

"You quite won them over! Of course your good looks are not a disadvantage. Will you marry me?"

She goggled at me. "Did you not hear a word I said?"

"Amanda, I do not believe you meant a word you said."

"I did too!"

"Who wrote that speech?"

She looked down into her glass, flustered, pink-cheeked. "I wrote the end part, about the woman dead at forty-three. I know her husband."

"And the rest? Mrs. Quinan?"

She nodded. I brimmed her glass.

"I'm glad you came," she said.

"I love you. I want to marry you. You would be as free as a bird. My mother would like one grandchild. Other than that I would not press my lusts upon you."

"But I would not have you without lusts!" She colored again.

The waiter appeared with oyster cocktails. These were followed by cold consommé, celery, green and black olives, and creamed shrimp.

Amanda was a great satisfaction as a dinner guest, exclaiming over each dish, complimenting me on my taste, raising her hands in amazement as more courses arrived: a mousse of foie gras, braised woodcock, alligator pear salad. Sauterne. Ices. Coffee.

Dinner at the Poodle Dog was only a dollar, but champagne was ten dollars a quart, and the wine added up.

"Oh, Cousin!" Amanda said. Her face was brighter than usual with fine wine. "Do you eat like this every evening?"

"Every evening when I have a beautiful cousin to celebrate," I said.

In this mood she was transported to my rooms on Sacramento Street for another glass of champagne. There a line of conversation ended with my being granted a number of kisses, and one wish. I wished to admire her pretty bosom. I was not to touch, however. I promised. Latches, hooks, and several layers of fabric were undone and parted and the marvel of the bosom revealed—small pale breasts with childlike pink nipples and a scattering of golden freckles over all. Amanda held her dress open for a split second, pink-faced and wrinkle-nosed, and then snapped the vision closed.

"There!" she said. "Now you must take me back to the hotel!"

....

One more grand dinner should do the trick, I thought in bed that night, *one of these evenings soon, at one of the other French restaurants—Marchand's, Tortoni's, Maison Doree, Maison Riche—those proud and scandalous eating and sinning establishments, with their live frogs in the windows, incredible menus, expensive wines, and plush upholstered "upstairs suites."*

For a start, I thought, *oysters Kirkpatrick, then frogs' legs a la poulette, and terrapin. Four courses and three varieties of wine should do it, and then back here for a bottle of Pommery. And dessert.*

The next step, then, the persuasion that kissing her pretty bosom was very little different from kissing her pretty face, of which there had been kissing aplenty. Further steps laid themselves out in orderly fashion.

I slept. I awoke with a start. A vast figure stood over me, a giant, an angel in white robes, crowned with silver spikes and holding up an enormous sword. The angel was so tall that its face was almost invisible, but the expression of extreme disapproval was evident. The sword did not move, merely glinting in a little light from the window, and the figure did not speak, but words formed themselves in my brain.

She is your cousin, your father's sister's daughter's child.

She is by no means the twenty-one she claims to be.

Despite her professions of Free Love she is a young and innocent girl, and probably a virgin.

I understood that the figure standing over me was my conscience.

I slept wakefully until gray dawn seeped in my window.

MONDAY, FEBRUARY 15, 1892

The next day I met Amanda in the tea shop next door to the Cyrus Hotel, where we sat across from each other at a tiled table with the pot and cups between us.

When I asked Amanda her true age, she colored prettily but did not respond.

"I don't believe you are twenty-one," I said.

"It is impolite to question a lady's age, Cuz."

"Are you eighteen?"

"I *was* eighteen."

"I believe you are a virgin."

"I most certainly am not!"

"How many times not a virgin, then?" All at once I was furious with jealousy instead of filled with anticipation at the thought of her surrender to me.

"That is none of your business!"

"But I am in love with you!"

"Oh, bosh! You just think I am available and so you

have been thinking about me in a way that you know you should not."

She was right. I had assumed she was available.

I perceived that she had attitudes and assumptions about me, maybe anti-male, certainly anti-marriage, maybe ironic, and maybe sympathetic.

CHAPTER THREE

KILL, v. t. To create a vacancy without nominating a successor.
— The Devil's Dictionary

TUESDAY, FEBRUARY 16, 1892

MURDER OF A DIVINE

HENRY DEVINE SHOT IN HIS STUDY

SHOCKING MURDER OF A POPULAR PREACHER

The Examiner *will investigate*

On a foggy morning Bierce and I, accompanied by Captain Chandler, the chief of detectives, and a patrolman in an eight-button uniform, were let into the Reverend Devine's study by a scared-looking colored man in a black suit. It was a large, airy room with south-facing windows and a city view, a desk, some horsehair leather furniture, and a couch. It had already been searched by Captain Chandler's men.

My eyes went first to the couch, which had a broad

triangle of vari-colored, fringed silk draped over it; and next to it the dark, pear-shaped stain on the rag rug beside the desk, where Henry Devine had bled to death from a shot in the heart.

Captain Chandler was pointing to it. He was a tall, gaunt-faced fellow with a fringe of chin whiskers. He did not speak much—he was deathly afraid of Bierce taking after him in "Prattle," which had driven his predecessor out of town, and he seemed worried that too many words might give Bierce something to work on. The patrolman was a tall, big-featured fellow with a hairy mole on his chin.

Bierce wore black with a high collar and a bed-of-flowers cravat, hat in hand. He frowned down at the stain on the floor as though envisioning the shooting.

"Anybody hear the shot?" he asked.

"The colored fellow," Captain Chandler said. "Expect he dithered a bit before he looked in. Then he saw the rev stretched out on the floor. Perpetrator went out that door there. There's an anteroom there, and a hallway to outside."

"Ladies," Bierce said, nodding, and Captain Chandler nodded also. There would be a discouraging number of leads to follow, some of which might involve people in high places.

"A revolver is usually not a lady's favorite weapon," Bierce said, and Chandler nodded again.

"Husbands," he said gloomily. He had a habit of twitching his fingers through his whiskers.

"Famous all over town," the patrolman said, gazing at the couch.

"And that door?" Bierce said.

The door revealed a closet, and inside I found four of the

brown robes, freshly pressed, and polished boots on a rack; all innocent enough.

Chandler was still considering husbands. "Case twenty some years ago," he said. "Miner named Edwards. English fellow seduced his wife while he was up on the Comstock. Killed the Britisher. Had an insanity plea all worked out, but the jury let him off for just cause."

"Do you think such a defense would hold these days, Captain?" I asked.

"Dunno."

"Just cause, I'd say," the patrolman said.

"I'm afraid the guilt of betrayed husbands is an assumption based on hearsay," Bierce said. "Is there some form of little black book?"

"No little black book were found, Mr. Bierce."

"Hearsay has it that at each of his sermons some numbers of his doxies were present. No doubt others had remained at home. Such a total presents a Herculean task of investigation, Captain Chandler."

Chandler nodded gloomily, tweaking his whiskers.

"At what hour did the shooting take place?"

"About ten P.M., says the butler-fellow. Devine was in here, somebody must've come in the anteroom entrance and done the job, and gone. Door left open."

"Ah!" Bierce said.

I returned to the closet to pat the pockets of Devine's robes. "Another rumor," I said. "He kept a supply of gold eagles in his pocket and jingled them together when he was nervous."

"Good bit to be nervous about, I'd say," the patrolman said, and received a reproving glance from Captain Chandler.

All the pockets were empty.

"No gold eagles found, Mr. Redmond," Captain Chandler said.

"Was there a wife?" Bierce asked.

"Died a couple of years ago back in Ohio, where Devine comes from," Chandler said. "There's some children that's left with his sister."

"How many children?" I asked, thinking of Amanda's story.

"Don't know that."

Bierce had moved over to examine the top of the desk. A large leather writing surface was adorned with a darker cross, and there was a cross also on a little stone box for ink bottles, and pens in a metal tube. It was a neat desk except for one curious object, a small decorated teacup with crimped edges and a flared blue handle, but no saucer. There were two beads in the cup.

Bierce plucked up the object and poured the beads into his hand. "Pearls," he said.

I gazed over his shoulder at the iridescent little globes.

"I wonder if these have to do with Devine's female preoccupations," Bierce said. "Can you tell if they are real ones, Captain?"

"I can find out, Mr. Bierce. There's a fancy box of them in one of the desk drawers, twenty-two in all."

Bierce found and examined the store of pearls with mutterings of interest.

"Pearls may have some significance in this matter," he said, restoring the fancy little mother-of-pearl box to its drawer.

"How's that, Mr. Bierce?"

"The Reverend Devine was ranged on the side of the Suffragists and Mrs. Quinan, whose three star performers are called the Trey of Pearls."

Captain Chandler frowned at this significance, and I felt a chill. Two pearls in a cup, and a box of them in a drawer.

"Bring that colored fellow in here," Captain Chandler said to the patrolman, who departed in a head-forward hurry.

....

The colored man's name was Deacon Robbins and he was so frightened that his complexion was more pale than brown. He knew nothing of the cup containing the pearls, or of the box of them. Members of the congregation often brought the Reverend Devine gifts. What other gifts? Flowers. They often brought flowers. What were the names of the members of the congregation who brought flowers? He couldn't remember. What of the stories that women came to the side door, and passed through the anteroom to join the reverend here? Often people came to pray with the Reverend Devine, certainly that was the truth.

"The truth I want, Robbins, is the name of the women that come here not to pray but to spread themself out on the couch there for the reverend's satisfactions!" Captain Chandler brandished a finger in Deacon Robbins's face. "Now, who was those women?"

Robbins gaped at him. In a hoarse whisper, he said, "Beg to differ with you, Cap'n, but women come to pray here with the reverend."

"Same thing?" Bierce said.

"Who was those women come to pray with the reverend, then?"

Robbins didn't know any names, except the lady who came to arrange the flowers, and the one who played the piano, and the one who led the choir, and Mrs. Kurtz, who swept out the chapel. He hadn't actually seen any of the Reverend Devine's callers.

"Privileged information," I said.

"You all better look into the Reverend Stottlemyer over at the All-Jesus Church on Washington Street," Deacon Robbins said, folding his arms. "He has made some threats against the Reverend Devine."

"Did he now?" Chandler said, plucking at his whiskers.

"Threats," Robbins said, nodding. "Says he would bring a bunch of vigilantes over here to Clay Street and clean us out."

"The Reverend Stottlemyer," Bierce said.

"Yes, sir. The Reverend Devine was tolerable upset about that."

"Stottlemyer is a pack of trouble I guess I will have to look into," Chandler said.

"You do that, Cap'n!" said Robbins, who had regained his sang froid.

"Get out of here," Chandler said, and Deacon Robbins departed.

"Mrs. Pleasant will have information on this matter," Bierce said to me.

"Need his black book, like you said, Mr. Bierce," Captain Chandler said.

"I'll talk with the women Robbins mentioned," Bierce said to him. "The lady who does the flowers, the pianist, the choir lady, and the chapel sweeper, Mrs. Kurtz. Can we view the body?"

"At the morgue," Captain Chandler said.

Before we left, Bierce wanted to see the church, which Reverend Devine's quarters adjoined. The great hall was empty and echoing, although the flower lady had been at work, for many vases exhibited sprays of blooms. Bierce regarded the ranks of pews and the platform, touching a finger to his chin.

We departed for the city morgue on Dupont Street.

....

On the slab the Reverend Devine looked smaller than I remembered him, striding across the platform in his brown gown, with his all-embracing arms raised. He had the face of an exhausted child. His eyes were sunken, his nose long with a cleft tip to it, his cheeks pale, the ringlets on either side of his face tangled. A sheet was drawn up to his throat, so the wound was not visible.

"He came to call on me after I had offered some opinions of him in 'Prattle,' " Bierce said. "Not to remonstrate, but to forgive. And where is your celebrated forgiveness now, Reverend Devine? Your vestments and canonicals? Where are your sermons and homilies, where the Divine love? If you were able to love your fellow man as well as his woman, perhaps you have been snatched off to paradise, with a splendid view of us sinners in the pit below."

"I went to his sermon on Sunday. He said sinners are the true Christians. And vice versa."

"Indeed!"

....

I was in Bierce's office when Mammy Pleasant came to call, her shawl making a kind of cowl over her dark old face that was sharp as a hatchet, her brown basket under her arm, large enough for carrying babies. That Mammy Pleasant farmed babies was one of the many myths—or realities—about her life. She entered with a slinking gait, like a cat mousing. Bierce was on his feet in an instant, for she was his great source of covert information, of both high and low degree.

She was his faithful informant because of poetry he had written in aid of the Fourteenth Amendment, and against the opponents of Negro suffrage, including the women Suffragists. And because Bierce treated her with respect.

She seated herself, nodding to Bierce, less cordially to me.

"Ah, Mrs. Pleasant!" Bierce said. "It is good of you to come. "May I ask if you can learn anything of the women who came to the Reverend Devine's side door to pray with him?"

"Many prayers," Mammy Pleasant said.

"There must be gossip."

"I will let you know what I find out."

"There's a colored fellow who was a kind of majordomo, Deacon Robbins. Is he really a deacon?"

"That is his proper name."

"The Reverend Stottlemyer," Bierce said. "A church over on Washington Street."

Mammy Pleasant was nodding. "Poison," she said.

"He'd made some threats, says Robbins. Disapproved of Devine. His ladies, I imagine."

"Disapproves of a good deal besides Devine," Mammy said. "Calls himself the Jesus-man. He has set himself as prime judge of conduct in this sinful city. Speaks of calling up the vigilantes again, clean out the parlor houses and cowyards and such. He is one that figures women is getting too uppity, for instance those Suffragist ladies that is going to march next month. He is on to that like a bearcat."

"*That* is interesting," Bierce said.

Mammy Pleasant looked hard at me with her dark, rather sinister face. "Mr. Redmond do know one of those Pearls of Madame Quinine pretty well," she said.

I could feel my face reddening. "She is my cousin," I protested.

"I will nose around, Mr. Bierce," Mammy Pleasant said, dismissing the subject. She had rearranged the position of the skull on the desk so that it gazed after her as she left us, basket under her arm.

"I had better look in at the All-Jesus Church," I said.

CHAPTER FOUR

MINISTER, n. An agent of a higher power with a lower responsibility.
—The Devil's Dictionary

TUESDAY, FEBRUARY 16, 1892

In Willie Hearst's grand office with windows looking up a sunny sweep of Montgomery Street, Willie sat at his desk straight-backed and narrow-shouldered, while Sam Chamberlain slumped in a chair beside the desk, monocled eye fixed on Bierce.

"It does seem a Gee Whiz story, Mr. Bierce," Willie said. "A popular, womanizing minister shot down in cold blood. By a husband of one of his mistresses, no doubt."

"Enough doubt to make it interesting," Bierce said. He and I were seated in a pair of straight chairs facing Willie's desk, with its large black-metal and polished-wood telephone mechanism.

"Such a multitude of suspects," he went on. "Does the *Examiner* really desire to pry into so many private and seamy lives?"

"One gathers that you do not, Ambrose," Sam said.

"I believe my poor opinion of the human race would be even more impoverished by such a search. Moreover, there are other aspects that interest Tom and me."

"And what would those be, Mr. Bierce?" Willie asked, his long, thin hands steepled together.

"Pearls," Bierce said. "Devine had a collection of pearls in a fancy box in a desk drawer, and he was known to keep a store of gold eagles in his vestment pocket—to rub together during an attack of nervousness. This collection is missing, by the way. The pearls in his desk drawer, and two of them in a small decorated cup on his desk, were real pearls and of some value."

Willie regarded him over his steepled hands; Sam had detached his monocle.

"The pearls are what intrigue me, not the squadrons of vengeful husbands whom Captain Chandler must seek out."

"There is also the matter of threats from a rival preacher on Washington Street," I said, to move the subject away from pearls.

Willie and Sam Chamberlain gazed at me as though they had become aware of my presence for the first time.

"Indeed, there may be powerful individuals involved," Bierce said, nodding.

"One might remember, however," Sam said, "when *Woodhull & Claflin's Weekly* revealed the sordid details of Henry Ward Beecher's amative adventures, it was those ladies who were prosecuted for the crime of publication—not Beecher for the sin of adultery."

I knew something of this. In New York City, Victoria Woodhull's scandalous newspaper had published the story of the lawsuit over Henry Ward Beecher's numerous adulteries, especially those with Theodore Tilton's wife. Woodhull and her sister, Tennessee Claflin, had been thrown into prison under the Comstock obscenity laws. The two had had to flee to England to escape further prosecution.

"San Francisco has no Anthony Comstock, praise be," Willie said, but I thought he would be pleased enough to get into a courtroom and front page battle over freedom of the press.

"I think you and Sam had better be very sure that you want to start a campaign against adultery in our churches, Mr. Hearst," Bierce said. "It may be that the Reverend Stottlemyer of the All-Jesus Church has already begun such, with a call for a return of vigilantism."

Sam Chamberlain and Willie Hearst glanced at each other. "The fellow who writes in the *Transcript* sometimes," Sam said.

The *Evening Transcript* was a trashy weekly that was a kind of organ for Protestant hellfire preachers ranting on the badness of most things, which made me very comfortable about my not-very-consistent attendance at Old St. Mary's, and reminded me of my determination to introduce Amanda to good Father Flanagan there.

Willie sighed. "Censorship is such a tiresome business," he said. He steepled his hands again, and gazed at Bierce over his fingertips. "Of course you must follow your instincts in this matter, Mr. Bierce."

"Thank you, Mr. Hearst," Bierce said.

When we had departed the proprietor's presence, Bierce said to me, "I must converse with your cousin, Tom."

"I will ask you to be gentle," I said.

WEDNESDAY, FEBRUARY 17, 1892

Amanda had shucked her Suffragist white dress with the slim black belt around her middle, which made her waist look spannable by a pair of hands, for a rather fancy plaid affair that presumed a bosom of more dimension than I knew it to be, and a large hat with felt lumps like fruit and a heavy fringe that flickered and convulsed when she turned her head from me to Bierce. Her pretty face was small and pale under the big hat.

We were lunching at the Palace Hotel in the noon brilliance streaming through the great skylights. Amanda sat with her hands clasped together before her, smiling nervously.

Bierce said, "You are aware, my dear, that your cousin and I are investigating the murder of the Reverend Devine?"

She wrinkled her nose and stretched her smile. "Yes, I know, Mr. Bierce. It is very sad. Henry Devine was a good man, and on our side."

"Tom and I were allowed to view his study, where the murder took place. On his desk was a little cup containing two pearls. There was a box of some twenty more in a desk drawer. I wonder if you have any idea what they might imply."

She gazed at him steadily. She made a motion with her hands as though washing them, and shrugged expressively.

Bierce continued: "I have asked to have this conversation because of the fact that you and your two colleagues have been referred to as the pearls of the suffrage movement."

"That is true."

"And you were acquainted with the Reverend Devine?"

"I was."

"I understand that you are a practitioner of Free Love. I must inquire if you were intimate with the Reverend Devine."

Amanda hesitated so long that I thought she had decided not to answer. Her eyes never left Bierce's. She said in a small voice, "Yes, I was, Mr. Bierce."

Her brown eyes in her flaming face flickered at me. "I expect it is what you wanted to know also, Cuz."

"I respect your truthfulness," I said.

"I thought you might have guessed it," she said to me. Then to Bierce, "It is true. I was one of *those.* He was a lovable man, but perhaps not so fine a man as I had thought him."

"You said the same thing once before, Amanda," I said.

"I had thought him a paragon of his gender, but he was not that."

"In what particular did he disappoint you, Miss Wilson?" Bierce said.

"He spoke of his wife with disrespect, whom he had worn out with her marital duties and placed in a hospital. That is a matter of some importance to me." She gave me a sharp glance.

I said I understood that.

"I am interested in the procedure at the Reverend Devine's study," Bierce said. "You went to the side door and entered a passageway, and knocked on a door there, is that correct?"

"There was a special knock, Mr. Bierce. Three quiet knocks, and a pause, then a fourth."

Our plump waiter appeared with our plates—Amanda's trout, Bierce's corned beef, my sand dabs. I gazed down at these without interest. Pilsners were brought for Bierce and me, tea for my cousin. I considered purchasing a revolver and heading for the morgue to shoot the Reverend Devine in the heart again, and I felt sympathy for the murderer, our quarry.

Bierce was off on a different tack. "Let us say that the Reverend Devine was a collector. In his desk was a collection of pearls. He also kept a number of gold coins in his pocket. Were you aware of this, my dear?"

"Oh, yes. I have heard the coins clinking."

"And the pearls?"

"I have been the recipient of pearls, Mr. Bierce." She lowered her face to tend to her trout. There was a silence.

"Gifts."

"So I thought of them at the time."

Bierce had omitted the fact that the Reverend Devine had also collected women. When Amanda raised her head she was blushing again.

"Why were there two pearls in a little cup on his desk, Miss Wilson?"

"I don't know."

"The two other young women also referred to as Pearls. Might one of them, or two of them, also be involved?"

"I do not think so," Amanda said.

I prickled my throat with a gulp of beer.

Bierce sighed and said, "Is there anything you can think of that might point to the murderer, my dear?"

Amanda shook her head so the fringe on her hat jiggled and bounced.

"Mr. Bierce, of course there was something about the procedure—the word you used—that reminded me that this happened very often, with other women as well as myself. But I have no idea who they might be."

I thought her very pretty, and wholesome, with the color in her cheeks and her little chin raised, she who had been one of the Reverend Devine's mistresses.

"Thank you for answering so honestly these painful questions, Miss Wilson," Bierce said.

"Thank you for this lovely lunch in this beautiful hotel, Mr. Bierce."

Another gift for another service, I was not pleased to think.

When the three of us parted after lunch I took Amanda home with me.

....

In my rooms she wept.

I said I was the one who should weep.

She drew herself up and patted her eyes with a handkerchief slipped from her sleeve.

"Marry me," I said. "Then you will be an honest woman!"

"I am an honest woman!"

"I know," I said. "That's why I should weep."

"Your Mr. Bierce is very cold."

"He has a difficult time with women, since he detests the gender but loves them individually."

"What bosh!"

"Probably," I said. "He is the most brilliant, wrong-headed man it is possible to conceive of."

"I didn't tell him everything!"

"But will you tell me?"

"No, I won't! A woman is allowed to have secrets."

"Not from the man who loves her."

"Oh, bosh, Cuz!" I saw that she had cheered up. "How you must hate me!" she said cheerfully.

"No."

"If you are not angry that I have had Free Love with Henry Devine, then you are not a proper genuine red-blooded American male!"

"Of course I am angry."

"Well, then!"

She flung herself into my arms and presented me with a number of uncousinly kisses before she took her leave, sweeping out the door with one last beguiling glance back at me.

Moments later it occurred to me that I had been flummoxed.

CHAPTER FIVE

PLAN, v. t. To bother about the best method of accomplishing an accidental result.

—The Devil's Dictionary

THURSDAY, FEBRUARY 18, 1892

In his arguments with Mrs. Atherton at the *Examiner* I had heard Bierce proclaim that the only fictional form in which the perfection of art could be achieved, as well as the effect of totality, was in the short story. Mrs. Atherton had published some four novels by this time, and she was having none of that. Novels were an imperfect form, no doubt of it, she had responded, but as to totality, the short story was to the novel as a sneeze to an aria.

Bierce replied that there was no doubt that the Cathedral of St. Peter's in Rome was a work of art, but how could it possibly be said that the city of Rome was a work of art? The only time a novel could be considered a work of art was when its covers were closed.

Both of them contradicted themselves, Bierce in "Prattle" and Mrs. Atherton in "Woman in Her Variety," and each of them disagreed with the other even when they agreed. Mrs. Atherton (in her column) advocated economic independence for women, touted divorce for loveless marriages, contraception against unwanted children, and bitterly protested the double standard. But she had recently devoted one whole column to fulminating against Free Love.

The argument today was in Bierce's office; I found Bierce seated with his back to the window, Mrs. Atherton standing statuesque in a gray silk dress, her proud profile set in warlike lines. She shook a finger at him from the other side of his desk, above the chalk-white skull. I watched from a straight chair by the door. Outside the office was the usual *Examiner* racket of voices raised, feet tramping in the corridor, names shouted.

Mrs. Atherton was indignant because Bierce did not wish to pursue, in our investigations, the women who had committed adultery with the Reverend Devine.

"Those despicable words, adultery and Free Love!" she said. "We simply cannot violate without terrible penalties hereditary laws that have become a part of our hearts' fiber! Why should they not be exposed?"

"You must be more temperate in your speech, Mrs. Atherton," Bierce said, leaning comfortably back. "Tom here is enamored of his cousin, one of the Suffragist Pearls, who is an advocate of Free Love."

Mrs. Atherton swung her beautiful head toward me. "Is that so, Mr. Redmond?"

"Yes it is, Mrs. Atherton."

"She is only parroting the opinions of that old frump Mrs. Quinan."

I held my peace.

"May I point out some inconsistencies in your arguments, Mrs. Atherton?" Bierce said. "You promote divorce for loveless marriages, and yet many religions would call succeeding marriages adultery, which you decry."

Mrs. Atherton retreated a step, breathing hard but smiling. "I have never known you to give anything but the back of your hand to *all* religions, Ambrose Bierce!"

She paced in the small office, swishing her skirts. She was a fine figure of a woman, with her wealth of fair hair massed above her marble features.

She said, "I see no reason why these silly females should be protected from their criminal foolishness!"

"Wisdom is the mother of compassion, Mrs. Atherton. It is an old Chinese saying."

"Nonsense, it is a new Biercian saying, which I will look forward to reading soon in 'Prattle.' May I point out certain inconsistencies in *your* arguments, Ambrose? You speak with utter scorn of the gray batter of the female brainettes, you speak of the list of female accomplishments as having been made by heaven considerately short, and yet in your grand compassion you will not pursue these very possibly guilty-of-murder females!"

"My dear Mrs. Atherton, why don't you pursue these guilty ones in their variety in 'Woman in Her Variety?' "

It seemed to me that Bierce, who was no doubt as interested in Mrs. Atherton's intimate flesh as he was in that of other women, was slightly fearful that she might be as intelligent as he was, that she might turn out to be as successful as he was, or even more so in her publication of novels. She in her turn was fearful of his censure, and desirous of his praise. At the same time she might be repelling his advances.

"And how does your cousin defend Free Love?" Mrs. Atherton asked, turning to me.

"She attacks marriage as slavery for women."

"It is for men as well," Bierce said.

"She describes someone she knows who has had six children

and five miscarriages, and died in a rest home while her husband pursued other women."

It was clear that this was the Reverend Devine's wife.

"Indeed!" Mrs. Atherton said.

"Please allow me to respond from Mrs. Atherton's writings," Bierce said. " 'Marriage is correlative with all that is commonplace. It is a prosaic grind that corrodes away life and soul and imagination. It is a dreary and infinite monotony.' "

"How flattering that you should memorize my words, Ambrose!"

She turned again to me and said, "Your cousin is not one of those ugly Suffragists, I take it, being a so-called 'Pearl'?"

"She is very pretty."

"Indeed she is," Bierce said. "And in most respects a very commendable young woman."

I recognized that Amanda was merely pretty while Mrs. Atherton was a beauty, but as far as I was concerned any dealings with Mrs. Atherton would involve a ten-foot pole, whereas merely kissing my cousin, even if she was an adultress and the proponent of a shocking doctrine, was very gratifying.

"I would be pleased to meet this young woman," Mrs. Atherton said. "I assume she is quite blatant in her personal life?"

"Not at all," I said. *Maybe not blatant,* I thought, *but kissy.*

"I would inform her that Free Love and adultery violate the oldest and most precious precepts of the human race!"

"In its grand variety," Bierce said, and Mrs. Atherton flounced out of the office with a rap of heels in the corridor outside Bierce's door.

"I believe Mrs. Atherton is incapable of a normal association with anyone of the opposite gender," Bierce told me.

"Her marriage was disastrous; George Atherton was an absolutely useless human being. He died on a sea voyage, you know, and they shipped him home to her encased in a barrel of brandy. What a thing to arrive at your door, with the drayman awaiting his payment!"

....

Mammy Pleasant arrived, bonneted and cloaked, and set her baby-farming basket on the floor beside her chair. She leaned forward over Bierce's desk to touch the skull, as though for luck. "I have some names for you to peruse, Mr. Bierce."

"Thank you, Mrs. Pleasant."

She handed him a list of names on a ruled sheet of paper.

"There are more that I don't know about."

Bierce looked at the list, then handed the sheet to me. One of the names stood out: Mrs. William Jaspers.

The others meant nothing to me.

Bierce said, "Those with husbands who might have done the deed, Mrs. Pleasant?"

She nodded and took the list from me, and pointed with a bony finger.

"Jaspers. He did it before."

"What do you mean, Mrs. Pleasant?" I asked.

"Back in the seventies. Left his wife in the City while he was on the Comstock, and a neighbor took advantage of her. Jaspers followed the fellow up to Nevada City, where he was staying in a rooming house, called him to the door, and shot him dead. Got away with it."

"Captain Chandler mentioned that," I said. "But I think he said the name was Edwards."

Mammy shrugged elaborately. There had been many assumed names in the Gold Rush, on the Comstock, and in California in general.

"Called him out and shot him," Bierce said, frowning. "It is almost too convenient. Any others that struck you, Mrs. Pleasant?"

"Carling. Thomas. Maybe Chase."

"Ah, Borden Chase," Bierce said. "He has a very pretty wife. And Mrs. Jaspers is evidently younger than her husband?"

"She is a young woman," Mammy Pleasant said.

"Is this list from Deacon Robbins?"

"Him and others."

"We are very grateful and will work from this. Thank you, Mrs. Pleasant."

"James Carling is the chairman of the board of directors of the God Is Love Church," Mammy Pleasant said.

"That is interesting," Bierce said. "He was the Reverend Devine's employer, you might say."

"Good friend," Mammy said. "Admired the Rev Devine a good deal. Stood up for him when there was that scandal last year; board of directors wanted to dismiss him."

Nodding, Bierce said, "Young woman claimed he had promised to marry her and reneged, wasn't it?"

"Name of Mary Belcher," Mammy Pleasant said. "She had letters. Thrown out of court by Judge Osborn that is well known not to give a female a square shake. Mr. Carling stood up for Devine before the board that was shocked about their minister in court."

"Anything on Stottlemyer?" I asked. I now recalled the Washington Street preacher as a very tall, skinny gent with flashing eyes, who had a great following of Jesus people, one of whom had once been a concern of Bierce's and mine.

"He is a real Trojan for working people up. It may be he comes from Stockton; maybe he got run out of town for some reason."

"I believe he writes for the *Transcript* on occasion," Bierce said. "No sense of what he may have been run out of town about?"

"I'll keep nosing," Mammy said, and rose. Bierce rose with her.

"We are very obliged to you, Mrs. Pleasant."

She nodded once in response, in her nod the absolute knowledge of where Bierce stood, and I stood, and she stood. She took her leave.

"Oh, what a tangled web," Bierce said, when we were alone. "I think we must employ Occam's Razor."

Get rid of the less essential essentials. Get rid of the less essential nonessentials, anyway. Jaspers loomed in the firmament like a dark star.

"Jaspers," I said.

"Let us consider how we shall approach Jaspers," Bierce said. "Who is a vitrolic and perhaps violent Grand Noble Humbug."

"That crazy preacher is another violent one. You don't suppose there's any danger to the Trey of Pearls from him, do you?"

Bierce spread his hands in a gesture of unknowing, sighed, and changed the subject. "It is important that I meet the Pearls and their brigadier," he said

"They have survived Occam's Razor, then," I said. "Shall we call on Mr. Jaspers first?"

....

The Cumberland Bank was at the corner of Montgomery and Sacramento streets, and Mr. Jaspers's office on the mezzanine, with mahogany paneling, leather chairs, and an embossed tin ceiling. With the Bull Clamper was a burly young man in a high collar, with a tugboat jaw and chin whiskers neatly cut to match those of Jaspers. He gave us a startled glance and rose; Jaspers leaned back in his chair.

"So, Bierce, have you changed your mind about the temperance ladies?"

"No, I have not," Bierce said. "We come on another matter."

The young man was introduced as Mr. Patchett, the cashier. He gestured for permission to depart, but Jaspers made a motion that a dog might have interpreted as "Stay!"

Jaspers waved Bierce and me to chairs with a similar arrogant motion. Beneath us was the bustle of the bank, and the rap and shuffle of shoe leather on a tiled floor. On Jaspers's desk was a thick green ledger.

"Mr. Jaspers, twenty years ago an Englishman named Oscar Larrikin was murdered. The man who shot him was named Edwards, which name has been changed to Jaspers."

"What's this about, Mr. Jaspers?" the young man said, glowering at us.

"Never mind it, Frank. It was bound to come up. Yes, that is true, Mr. Bierce, although it does seem a bit rude to come up here and charge me with murder in front of an employee."

"As you say, the matter was bound to come up. I hope you will correct me if my facts are not precise. You were mining on the Comstock, leaving your young wife in a rooming house on Mission Street—"

"Yes, yes," Jaspers said. "Where she was seduced by Oscar Larrikin. I sought her lover out and shot him."

"And the jury decided you had just cause," I said.

"Indeed I had!"

Patchett glared at me.

"She was a fool and a wanton," Jaspers said. In his face old outrage presided like varicose veins. "I shot the English bastard. I'm not one to brag on it, but I surely don't regret it!"

"You did change your name," I said.

"You did not find many true names on the Comstock in those days."

He leaned back and took a deep breath, and for the first time I thought he might be feeling some strain. "In fact, gentlemen, Edwards was a little too well known because of the shooting, and I was glad to leave him behind me."

"What is all this about, Mr. Jaspers?" Patchett said in a voice of controlled fury.

"It is all right, Frank. We are all friends here, are we not, Mr. Bierce?"

Bierce said, "What happened to Mrs. Edwards after the trial?"

"I divorced her. She was a whore; she confessed her shame to me. She died, years ago."

"Was there issue?" Bierce asked.

"Not by me. There may have been by later men, later on. I have no knowledge of that."

"Where did she die, Mr. Jaspers?" I asked.

"In the foothills, I believe. Is this interrogation leading somewhere, gentlemen?"

"We are interested in that old case," Bierce said. "And thought it more forthright to ask you the details, rather than looking them up in the newspaper archives."

"Would you know when she died, Mr. Jaspers?" I asked.

"Years ago. I don't know precisely, no. Her name was Dora McCall, and she came from the town of Colfax on the Central Pacific line, in the foothills. Will that suffice you?"

"The British Consul did not feel the judgment was a proper one."

"Made some fuss, yes."

"The reason you shot Larrikin was that you had discovered your wife's infidelity?"

"Yes, yes, that is correct."

"Mr. Jaspers, I will be pleased to usher these gents out, if you wish!" Patchett said.

"In a moment, Frank. I'm sure we are almost finished here. Anything else, Mr. Bierce?"

"You have since married again, Mr. Jaspers?"

"I have. A lovely young woman. What could possibly be the reason behind this line of questioning, Mr. Bierce?"

"Don't you know?" Bierce said, and we rose to go.

Patchett continued to glower. He had picked up the big green ledger and now held it against his chest. Jaspers did not rise with us.

"Is it on behalf of your temperance-lady friends, Mr. Bierce?"

"I can assure you that it is not," Bierce said.

CHAPTER SIX

GARTER, n. An elastic band intended to keep a woman from coming out of her stockings and desolating the country.

— The Devil's Dictionary

THURSDAY, FEBRUARY 18, 1892

It appeared a scene of heaven from a bad stage play, this room under the eaves of the hotel, where a number of seemingly airborne angelic figures swathed in white material were ranged at various removes. One attendant angel, an older woman with nose-pincher glasses, stood at a lectern reading to her auditors, no doubt Suffragist doctrine: Mrs. Quinan.

Bierce and I stood just inside the door, gaping at this monochromatic scene, until one of the white-garbed figures rose and hurried toward us—Amanda. I realized that the others were sewing costumes.

Amanda curtsied to Bierce and bussed me on the cheek, and turned to introduce Mrs. Quinan. Mrs. Quinan observed us coldly as this procedure took place. She was holding a thick volume with a finger marking her place in it.

"I see that you are reading from *War and Peace*, Madame," Bierce said.

"How do you do, Mr. Bierce, Mr. Redmond. Yes, I am. It is a splendid novel."

I thought Bierce might speak of this particular novel as having covers too far apart, but he only bowed.

"Miss Wilson has spoken of you," Mrs. Quinan said. "Are you here as friends or otherwise?"

"Friendly otherwise, Mrs. Quinan," Bierce said.

"They are here to ask some questions of Miss Prout and Miss Robinson," Amanda said.

Bierce identified us as investigating the death of the Reverend Devine.

"Questions concerning the frightful demise of our friend Henry Devine are welcome," Mrs. Quinan said. She had a way of pronouncing her words individually, as though she were reciting from some text inside her head. She turned to beckon, and two more of the angelic figures arose.

"We are sewing dresses for the parade," Amanda said.

"There is a great deal of white material," I said.

"It is the color of purity," Amanda said, straight-faced. "The yellow ribbons identify our cause."

Miss Prout wore a blue-and-white scarf tied over her hair. She was darkly beautiful, with a nervous habit of working her hands together, and she was as slender as Amanda, with the black belts narrowing their waists. Miss Robinson had blue eyes set so far apart they seemed almost to be on the sides of her head. She had a sweet, very young face.

Mrs. Quinan ushered us into an adjoining room, where we seated ourselves, the three young women in a row on a sofa, Mrs. Quinan standing beside them.

"I must speak of Free Love, as it concerns the murder of Mr. Devine," Bierce said.

I was surprised that all heads turned to regard Amanda, whose pretty cheeks reddened.

"Miss Robinson and I are not Free Love," Miss Prout proclaimed.

My cousin faced Bierce defiantly, chin up, while Mrs. Quinan gazed down on her Pearls, book in hand.

"On Mr. Devine's desk was a little painted cup," Bierce said. "In this cup were two pearls. It might be construed that these refer to you young women, Miss Prout and Miss Robinson. I must ask if either of you two had entered into a relation with Mr. Devine."

"I certainly had no relation with Henry Devine!" Miss Prout said.

Miss Robinson was shaking her head, white-faced.

"You were all acquainted with Mr. Devine, however," Bierce said.

"He was our great friend," Mrs. Quinan said. "His demise is a disaster for the cause."

"So you might think his demise was brought about by an enemy of the cause?" Bierce said.

"Indeed I would!" Mrs. Quinan had iron-gray hair and a hard-jawed face with cold eyes, but a full-lipped mouth.

"He was a fine man," Miss Prout said in her firm voice. "But his relations with our gender were not above criticism."

"He was a very generous man," Miss Robinson said.

"He was generous with his pearl collection, I understand," I said. "I wonder if you were presented with one."

Amanda looked daggers at me. Miss Robinson frowned. "No, I was not," she said.

"Miss Prout?"

"I don't know what you are talking about, Mr. Redmond."

"Henry Devine may not have been above criticism in his relations with our gender, Emmiline," Mrs. Quinan said reprovingly, "but it was he and a few other great spirits like him who helped us to forge the priceless tool of liberty, which in time will free us from the shackles of the centuries!"

We had been the recipients of a speech. I noticed that the three Pearls watched their mistress with respect as she enunciated her lines, to which it must have been especially difficult for Bierce not to respond.

"Of course that is very true, Mrs. Quinan," Miss Prout said.

"Would you be willing to specify as to enemies of the cause, Mrs. Quinan?" Bierce said.

"Are you not one, Mr. Bierce?"

"Certainly not in the way of physical violence, Madam."

"This E Clampus Vitas person has threatened violence."

"Mr. Jaspers," I said.

"There is a preacher—" Miss Prout said. "A nasty-minded, pestiferous brute."

"Stottlemyer," I said.

"I believe that is his name."

"We have our supporters," Amanda said. She was the prettiest of the three. Miss Prout, though she might be considered beautiful with her expressive dark eyes and white hands working at each other when she spoke, had a certain hardness around the mouth and a peppery manner of speech. Miss Robinson, the Bird Girl, did not seem to have many thoughts in her head, although she was a charming presence with her otherworldly eyes and her dark hair done up in tight braids.

"My cousin, for one," Amanda went on. "You *will* help to guard us from the fearful Clampers, won't you, Cuz?"

"Indeed I will!" I said. Mrs. Quinan was frowning at Amanda, who sucked in her chin, abashed.

"And will Mr. Bierce also?" Miss Robinson wanted to know.

"I will certainly be on hand for this considerable event,"

said Bierce, who was neither a bulwark of the Suffragist cause, nor a Clamper.

"I don't believe Mr. Bierce can be counted on in our support, Gloria," Mrs. Quinan said.

"No counting Mr. Bierce—?" Miss Robinson said, her face contorted into unfortunate facial gestures that were meant to be amusing.

She stopped as though she'd been slapped when Mrs. Quinan said, "Gloria!"

"I will address myself particularly to Mr. Bierce," Mrs. Quinan said. Again she spoke in lecturese: "The first tiny silver tinkle of women's equality and enfranchisement began to sound at Seneca Falls, so many years ago now. But that tiny and primitive toy has become a mighty brazen bell whose determined clamor fills the world! What do you say to that, Mr. Bierce?"

"Powerful words, Mrs. Quinan! This meeting has been an education for Mr. Redmond and me. We do wish, however, that there was some information about the Reverend Devine that would be helpful to this investigation."

"I am sorry that we have no more advice for you," Mrs. Quinan said, with a motion of her hand that might have indicated to the three that they were to say no more.

It seemed remarkable to me that she had made no effort to win Bierce over to the Suffragist side, for his comments in "Prattle" carried much weight.

"We thank you for the mention of Mr. William Jaspers of E Clampus Vitas, and of the Reverend Stottlemyer," Bierce said, rising. "Come along, Tom. We must let these ladies return to their labors and novel reading."

So we departed, leaving the four of them. It seemed that Mrs. Quinan exerted a strict dominance over her Pearls, even Amanda, who were not allowed to bid us farewell.

....

Outside, we strode along sunny, windy Market Street, among the crowds of cloth-capped and tall-hatted men holding on to their hats, big-hatted and scarf-headed women, beggars, a match girl, and a paper boy, in the racket of passing carriages, buggies, drays, and horse cars, that constant San Francisco sound of multitudinous hooves on paving stones merged into a kind of low thunder.

"That is a woman who would confirm, in the enemies of her cause, the rightness of their enmity," Bierce said.

I agreed with him.

"You must extricate your pretty cousin from her power!"

"I'm trying to marry her."

"That would seem to conflict with Miss Wilson's obsession. If it is *her* obsession and not merely that of her Svengali."

I felt argumentative.

"You say you have heard the Pearls in full voice," Bierce said. "The message of your cousin is Free Love; what is that of Miss Prout?"

It had been a kind of feminist general view.

"And Miss Robinson?"

"Does bird calls, and sang 'The Battle Hymn of the Republic.' "

"Mrs. Quinan herself did not speak?"

"Only to introduce them with a poem."

"She has induced them to carry her message because they are young and handsome, and she is only another cast-iron feminist with a chilly eye and a powerful embonpoint. She is performing a clever manipulation."

"You speak of her as though she were the enemy," I said.

"I believe she is. And we are hers. You also, Tom."

"I hope not," I said.

"It is Mr. Jaspers who interests us now. Shall we call upon Captain Chandler?" he said, not knowing that Captain Chandler had already sent a patrolman to bring William Jaspers to the police station to be interviewed.

CHAPTER SEVEN

REVELATION, n. A famous book in which St. John the Divine concealed all that he knew.

—The Devil's Dictionary

THURSDAY, FEBRUARY 18, 1892

Preceded by his considerable belly, the Bull Clamper arrived with a tall policeman, plug-hatted and frock-coated, with shiny boots treading the boards of Captain Chandler's office, where Bierce and Chandler and I waited.

"May I inquire what this is about, Captain?" Jaspers said. "Ah, Bierce, you are here, are you?"

"Mr. Bierce and Mr. Redmond are here at the behest of the *Examiner* newspaper," Chandler said. He had assumed a queer head-ducked posture, as though evading bullets over the parapet. "We are investigating the murder of Reverend Devine."

"Ah!" Jaspers said, and plumped himself down in the chair the patrolman proffered.

"Your wife was friendly with Mr. Devine, was she not?" Chandler said. He remained standing, with the rest of us seated in a rough semicircle around him. Behind him was a window revealing the courtyard a story below, and a bum sprawled asleep on a stone bench.

"She was, Captain. She is a religious-inclined woman. He prayed with her."

"You are aware, Mr. Jaspers," Bierce said, "that praying with the Reverend Devine is regarded as a euphemism for other activity."

The Bull Clamper's small blue eyes glared at Bierce. "I am well aware of that, Mr. Bierce. It was certainly not the case with my wife, however. You may be assured of that, Captain," he said, swinging his ponderous head toward Chandler.

"Our interest, Mr. Jaspers," Chandler said, "is in a case twenty years ago, in 1871 in fact—"

"No need to recount all that, Captain. I've been through this with Mr. Bierce. My first wife was a fool. Oscar Larrikin took advantage of her, and I shot him."

"You will, no doubt, Mr. Jaspers, understand that we might see this as a parallel situation."

"I see no parallels, sir!"

"Mr. Jaspers," Bierce said. "It is commonly said that each of Mr. Devine's sermons was attended by a fair number of his mistresses. His career as a womanizer certainly matches that of Henry Ward Beecher, some years ago. Surely that would satisfy you as to the importance of these questions."

The Bull Clamper's eyes seemed to grow smaller still, and he moved his head from side to side like a raccoon surrounded by enemies. "I will not have my wife maligned!" he said.

Chandler protested weakly, fingering his chin whiskers.

Bierce said, "You are certain, then, that your wife's meetings with Devine were theological rather than adulterous?"

"I am, sir!" Jaspers roared.

"Pearls," I murmured to Bierce.

"Tell me, sir," Bierce said. "Did Devine present your wife with pearls? He was known to keep a store of them and pass them out to the devoted."

"I am certain not," Jaspers said. He leaned back in his chair, as though trying to show himself at ease. "She would have told me."

"You and your wife have perfect confidence, then?" Bierce said. "I believe that is very rare."

"I have a rare wife," Jaspers said.

"And how does she feel about the Clamper position on the suffrage march?"

"She is in perfect agreement with the Clamper position. She has nothing but contempt for that Monstrous Regiment of Women."

"That would have put her at odds with Mr. Devine, then, would it not?" Bierce said.

The scowl clamped itself on Jaspers's face again. "She accepted the man's theological position, Mr. Bierce. That does not mean she accepted his suffrage and feminist positions."

Chandler was looking frazzled; Jaspers, of course, was an important man in the City.

"Well then, Mr. Jaspers—" he started, but Bierce interrupted.

"It is well known, Mr. Jaspers, that you are an enemy of the Suffragist cause, while the Reverend Devine was its great friend. Now we learn that he often prayed with your wife, but that she agreed with your position on Suffragists, not his. I wonder if there is anything we should conclude from this."

Jaspers ducked his head into his shoulders again and glowered at Bierce. "Nothing that I can see, sir!"

"What if, with his heaven-sent powers of persuasion, he had persuaded her to change her mind?"

"I can promise you that he did not!"

"What if he had in fact persuaded her to march in the Suffrage Parade, along with Mrs. George Hearst and many other socially prominent women in San Francisco? You would then look rather a fool in your opposition, Mr. Jaspers, and I wonder if your rage would then have descended upon your wife, or on the devil who had caused her to betray you?"

Chandler was regarding Bierce goggle-eyed, but I saw what Bierce was after.

"Why, I'd—!" Jaspers raised a clenched fist, and then, just as quickly, controlled himself. But he roared, "This is damned nonsense, Bierce! I have told you I will not stand for my wife to be maligned here!"

"All I wanted to know," Bierce said, "was the degree of your anger upon learning that your wife had betrayed you. We do, after all, know the degree in that case from twenty years ago."

....

I was assigned to write the piece on the past crime of William Jaspers for Sam Chamberlain's rewrite, but, fortunately as it turned out, it was an evening for the monthly dinner with my father, the gent, down from Sacramento for the day on Southern Pacific Railroad business. We always met at Malvolio's Restaurant on Kearny Street.

"The Bull Clamper!" my father said, seated opposite me in the warmth and delicious smells, surrounded by white napery and crystal glasses, and waiters in black with white arm napkins. My father's black chin whiskers were shot with white, and his napkin was tucked into his collar. He did like his food.

"I knew him on the Comstock. Edmonds, he called himself. Maybe it was Edwards. Married to a chit of a girl he left alone in the City here, and she got herself seduced."

"Englishman named Larrikin."

My father noisily ingested a radish, nodding.

"Well, he did love that girl. He'd talk about her! Sixteen

years old. That was the way to handle women, he said, marry 'em young and bring 'em up right. Let 'em know who's in charge. All that sort of twaddle. Talk your arm off. Then he went down to the City and next thing we know he was on trial for murder. Found out what had happened, tracked Larrikin to a boarding house up in the Mother Lode, and shot him dead. Jaspers then turned himself in to the sheriff there. It was in the papers. First we knew his name was really Jaspers. Will Jaspers, is it?"

"Will Jaspers divorced his wife then?"

"So I understand. Poor little thing didn't know whether she was coming or going. Come back to Sacramento. I knew of her there. She was from up near Colfax originally. Dora McCall. I believe she was a professional woman for a while, then she got married, but that didn't work out, and she come down with the consump. Died of it."

"Can you remember the name of her husband?"

"I'll think of it. He was a gambler, I believe, no sort of fellow at all."

The waiter brought steaming plates of pasta, lovely smells settling in happily along the nostrils. My father sat straight-backed, gazing down at his plate with a dazed expression of anticipation, spoon in one fist, fork in the other, both upright like guardians at the gate.

As I understood him, my father was a rascal by nature, employed by a rascally corporation, the Railroad, which controlled California. The state was run from the SP headquarters on Townsend Street in San Francisco. In his status as the boodler who passed out cash money to senators and representatives for correct votes on matters affecting the Southern Pacific, he naturally disapproved of Bierce, who fulminated against the railroad monopoly.

As a member of the True Blue Democracy Party in the City, I heartily disapproved of the dominance of the railroad in the State of California. When I'd protested, "Well, it shouldn't!" my father had said, "Son, we are not talking about *shouldn't,* we are talking about *is.* The SP Railroad *is!*"

"Had Dora McCall no children?" I asked.

He held his loaded fork two inches from his mouth, frowning. "Don't know that."

He chewed and swallowed and wiped his lips with his napkin, and then said, "What's it all about?"

I told him about the murder of the Reverend Devine, but of course he knew all about that already.

"Jaspers's wife prayed with Devine a good deal. Bierce thinks praying with Devine meant something else."

My father wiped his lips again. "So you and Bierce are detecting this business?"

That was about right. "Young wife," I said.

"I guess he didn't bring this one up all that right, either."

"Were you ever a member of E Clampus Vitas?" I asked.

"Just about everybody in my time tippled with those fellows, son. Nothing to it. There's just drinking whisky and some good fellowship. Jaspers was a loud-mouth fellow, always telling people how to do everything a better way than they was doing it. Widders and orphins! The fact is that Clampers just don't do much of anything but drink and joke."

"Jaspers was going to. There's a Suffrage March along Market Street coming up, and he swore the Clampers would wreck it."

My father clucked deep in his throat. "Isn't that just like a fellow that would let his poor divorced wife starve to death for her sins?"

"Did she starve to death?"

"Reduced circumstances, anyway. Cast off, consumptive, and all forlorn."

"Parallel circumstances also."

"Yes, I see," my father said. We sipped the good Chianti. He snapped his fingers. "Morton," he said. "Benny Morton. That was the fellow married her. So, does Bierce think Jaspers did the same again?"

"He thinks it is too obvious."

"Ha!" my father said. "That'd be like him, Almighty God Bierce."

We bent to our suppers.

....

"Your mother is still hoping to be a grandmother, son," my father said a little later. "Before it is too late."

"When's too late?"

"You know the way she talks."

"As a matter of fact, I've put a bid in."

"A good Catholic?"

"Maybe Protestant, but a cousin."

He stared at me. "You don't mean Lolly's oldest girl?"

"I guess I do."

"It would break your mother's heart!"

"Hers or mine."

"You have to have a dispensation for a cousin!" He looked frowningly concerned. "Why, Tom, I believe she's a rather wild young woman."

"I love her," I said.

Still, as always, he was a fount of knowledge, and the next day I consulted *The Call* of September 20, 1871, for the account of the murder of Oscar Larrikin in Nevada City, and October 27 for the trial. I wrote my piece and consulted with

Sam, who wanted to know more of the sad fate of Dora McCall Jaspers. So I rode the SP to Sacramento to confer with my friend Jimmy Harrow at the *Sacramento Bee*, and his friend Parson Jones, who was familiar with the Edwards murder case. The trial took place in Superior Court in Sacramento with a Mr. Rogers, the lawyer for the defense, prepared to prove that Edwards/Jaspers had become mentally unbalanced and not responsible for his actions when he had discovered that his beloved wife had succumbed to the wiles of a clever English seducer. But there was no need, for the jury was unanimously in favor of freeing the accused. All this happened in 1871.

Jaspers divorced his wife Dora for just cause the following year.

In 1880, Jaspers came into a good deal of money from investment in mining stocks; Dora sued for participation, as some of the stocks had been purchased when she and Jaspers were still married, but the case was decided against her. My informant pointed out that Judge Henry had, like Edwards, been a miner on the Comstock.

Dora's descent was inexorable. She resided in a house of ill repute in Sacramento, and she married a gambler named Benjamin Morton, who abused and deserted her. She returned to her parents' home in Colfax, her mother being still alive, but she was suffering from tuberculosis brought on by her hard times, and she died in a nearby sanitarium.

Jones thought there had been a son by Benny Morton, but the child had disappeared and might also have suffered from tuberculosis.

I wrote a long piece for Sam Chamberlain, who cut and rewrote it to engender pity for the poor woman, who had, after all, been only seventeen when she had practiced Free

Love, and had been in effect sentenced to death by her husband's vengefulness. William Jaspers was not afforded much sympathy, and I had a good idea that his vengeful mood might be reinstated.

There was no mention of the Devine murder, under the headline that implied it:

A PARALLEL MURDER?

SATURDAY, FEBRUARY 20, 1892

I was in my office reading the published edition when Jaspers barged in the door and smacked the paper out of my hands with a sweep of his arm. His glinting blue eyes in his red badger face glared at me. Behind him in the doorway was the young man Patchett with a jaw like a tugboat. When I tried to get to my feet, Jaspers shoved me in the chest so I staggered back against the wall and down into my chair again. "You damned skunk!" he shouted.

"Let me at him, Will!" Patchett said, and shouldered past Jaspers to grab me by the collar. When I swung a fist at him he knocked my arm up over his head. I ducked as he swung at me.

"Desist!" a voice said. It was Bierce, his revolver aimed at Patchett.

"Just a minute here—" Jaspers said.

"Unhand this gentleman," Bierce said.

Patchett did not relinquish his grip on my collar.

"I am aimed at your neck, young man," Bierce said. "If I fire your jugular will be severed and you will strangle on your own blood."

I was unhanded.

"Out!" Bierce said. Patchett obeyed, throwing his legs out mutinously to each side, but Jaspers lingered. He pointed a finger at Bierce.

"This is war, Bierce!" he said. "I do not lose wars!"

He lumbered out. Bierce pocketed his revolver.

I thanked him.

"We have indication that Jaspers is a gentleman subject to uncontrollable fits of temper," he said.

CHAPTER EIGHT

INJURY, n. An offense next in degree of enormity to a slight.
— The Devil's Dictionary

SATURDAY, FEBRUARY 20, 1892

In the hack headed south of Market Street Mammy Pleasant was silent. When she had nothing to say she said nothing. Her crinolines crinkled when she moved, she had her basket on her lap, she smelled of violets. Her sharp-featured, brown, old face peered straight ahead. It occurred to me that she carried her empty basket to confound all those who told stories about her.

It had been raining in little squalls all morning, rattling now on the buggy's bonnet, and chilly as well. I had turned the collar up on my overcoat, and Mammy wore a dark green cloak with a hood from which her hard face gazed out, as from an ambush.

What she had had to say was that the Trey of Pearls was in danger. A clairvoyant acquaintance of hers would provide me with the evidence. Bierce had found an excuse for not accompanying us. He did not believe in clairvoyance or spirit guides. I, however, was concerned with the welfare of my cousin.

....

There was a decreasing traffic of drays and buggies as we headed south on a muddy street, under low clouds. This was the route south out of town the banker William Ralston had taken from his offices at the Bank of California to his mansion in Belmont, thundering along four-in-hand behind his matched team, applauded by all as San Francisco's grandest capitalist and the builder of the Palace Hotel, until the crash of '76, which wiped out his fortune and his credit. His financial friends either deserted or betrayed him and he was found drowned after a swim in the Bay.

We passed a quartet of men with greasy gunnysacks folded over their shoulders, two with dark leather caps. They covered their heads with the gunnysacks as another squall rattled on the buggy's top.

Mammy directed the driver into a muddy lot between brick structures, into a harsh, sickening smell from the slaughterhouse next door. At the far end of the lot was a box-topped wagonette with black curliqued words on the side:

MME. STARR, PSYCHIC

Mme. Starr was a hugely fat, hard-breathing woman, who invited us up rickety steps with gestures of hospitality. Inside, in semi-darkness, she helped me off with my coat and Mammy her cloak. A redolence of incense battled the slaughterhouse stench. Mme. Starr sank back into a cushioned chair with cut-off legs, while Mammy and I seated ourselves on stools facing her across a round table. Mme. Starr lit a candle in a silver holder, and I inhaled a whiff of sulfur from the match. The light flickered over her greasily gleaming face, her jaw wreathed with chins, her forehead with straggly curls.

"This young man is cousin to one of the Suffragist young ladies," Mammy said.

Mme. Starr wheezed asthmatically and nodded more times than seemed necessary. "Mr. Randolph has warned me," she said. She had a soft voice with a hard edge to it.

I asked who Mr. Randolph was.

He was her friend on "the other side."

"He speaks to me often of the women's movement; he is very interested. He knew Mrs. Stanton, Mrs. Mott, and Miss Anthony when he was on this side. He is partial to their cause."

"What does he say endangers the Trey of Pearls?"

"The— pardon?"

"Miss Wilson, Miss Prout, and Miss Robinson."

"He believes it is gunshot danger."

"Have you found out more?" Mammy said.

"That is all he has said, Mrs. Pleasant."

"You said he had found a way of proving it to you."

"I will show you—if he is here. Mr. Randolph?" she said in a different voice.

"He is the son of John Randolph, you understand," Mammy whispered to me behind her hand. "He is her guide. He sought her out years ago."

"Mr. Randolph!" Mme. Starr said, more loudly.

The flame of the candle flickered to one side as though someone had waved a fan at it.

I supposed Mme. Starr had managed this somehow, unseen by me.

She produced a deck of cards from beneath the tabletop. "Now, Mr. Randolph, if you will help me—"

She shuffled and reshuffled the deck between her fingers, on which the stones in her rings glinted in the light. With a sudden motion she flicked the cards in a broad arc across the tabletop. One card detached itself and lay alone. Breathing hard, Mme. Starr turned it over. It was the three of hearts.

I could think of several ways this trick might have been managed. But why would Mme. Starr bother? I peered into the darkness, past her, for a sign of Mr. Randolph.

Mme. Starr gathered the cards and shuffled them again. She threw them out with the same gesture. This time the odd card was the queen of spades.

It was suddenly chilly in the wagonette.

"How by gunshot, Madame Starr?" Mammy Pleasant said.

Taking long breaths, as though she had been engaged in heavy labors, Mme. Starr gathered the cards once more, shuffled again, at greater length, and flung the deck out again. This time two cards separated themselves. Turned over, they proved to be a pair of fours, spade and club.

.44 caliber.

I was frightened against my will.

"Is it the Clampers?" I asked.

Mme. Starr peered at me nearsightedly. She seemed almost in a trance. I repeated my question.

"Mr. Randolph?" she called. "Mr. Randolph?" This time the candle did not flicker.

"If you will keep after him about this," Mammy said.

"Yes," I said.

"Mr. Bierce would not come to observe," Mammy Pleasant said to me, sounding pleased.

"He does not believe," I said.

"But you do, Mr. Redmond?"

"Maybe I do," I said.

"You will maybe then give Mme. Starr three dollars."

I produced the coins from my pocket and spread them out on the table.

....

When I described the session to Bierce he sat facing me across his desk with the tips of his fingers pressed together and a knot of disapproval between his eyebrows.

"I was convinced then," I said. "I don't know if I still am."

"Unfortunately," Bierce said, "Captain Chandler has reported much the same message."

"From where?"

"He would not divulge the source. But at least the police will be aware."

"That is not much comfort," I said.

"Gunshot."

"Yes."

"It is a tenuous connection with the death of Devine."

"Yes," I said. His desk skull gaped at me, implying death like the queen of spades.

"No doubt you will be keeping a close watch on your cousin."

"Yes," I said.

"She and you and I have been invited to breakfast tomorrow at Mrs. Atherton's apartment on Nob Hill. At ten o'clock."

"We will happily accept. I have a ballgame at two."

"Ballgame?"

Bierce was perfectly aware that I played baseball for the Firemen most Sundays. "Baseball," I said.

"Ah, yes."

"In fact, the Firemen are playing the San Francisco Clampers."

"That is interesting," Bierce said. "Considering your encounter of yesterday. Where will this take place?"

"The playing fields out Market Street."

"And will your pretty cousin attend?"

"I hope so. I hope to keep an eye on her."

"First, however, breakfast at Mrs. Atherton's. I suspect she intends to take issue with your cousin's romantic ideal of Free Love."

"She'll find Amanda a tartar on the subject."

"An interesting Sunday," Bierce said.

"That's not all of it," I said. "I'll also attend the early morning service at the All-Jesus Church on Washington Street."

"Shall we now tread the Saloon Route?" Bierce said. "It is close to that time."

....

Bierce and I set out among crowds of gents in top hats, saluting each other with their canes or a finger to a hat brim, and cloth-capped others, rowdy or circumspect, in the Saturday evening democratic celebration among the saloons along Market Street. The clouds had drifted away and stars were out. No doubt this crowd of drinkingmen was salted with members of E Clampus Vitas, as when we had encountered the Grand Noble Humbug in Blessington's Saloon two weeks ago.

I was ill-prepared to defend my story on the solid citizen and Bull Clamper William Jaspers, since it seemed craven to respond that the editor had set an entirely different slant on the story than had been initially written.

The saloon called The Crystal was named for its crystal chandeliers and large oil paintings on the walls, some of partially clad ladies, one of deer drinking at a brown forest pond, one of a brace of dead rabbits with a shotgun.

Here we encountered Marshall McGee, a fat little fellow in a checked suit, with a beard so short it looked as though he had only neglected to shave this week, and a balding head. His column in the *Chronicle*, "Ponyfeathers," was a poor imitation of "Prattle," and much concerned with city gossip. Although he followed Bierce's example of punishing folly, cant, hypocrisy, and civic unworth, he didn't seem to be throwing his thunderbolts from real indignation, only from an observance of his master Mike DeYoung's prejudices.

He had a way of slanting his face at you with a rubber-lipped sneer, as though starting a corkscrew.

"So, Bierce!" he said, as if about to issue some grand condemnation for malpractice.

"So, McGee!" Bierce responded.

"So you and Tom Redmond here are running another murder investigation for Willie Hearst."

"For the *Examiner*, as we like to say at the *Examiner*."

"Mike DeYoung leaves police investigations to the police."

"Mike DeYoung will no doubt presently come to copy *Examiner* practice in this as in many other things."

"Ha ha!" McGee said. "The *Chronicle* hasn't had its staff doing stunts all over the Bay yet!" He screwed his face at me as though he had my number.

"A very refreshing hour in the Bay," I said.

"So you wrote that piece about the old Larrikin murder," he said.

"I did."

"Don't imagine Will Jaspers was much pleased."

"Not much."

"Took after him in 'Prattle' on the Suffragist thing, didn't you?" he said, screwing his face toward Bierce.

Bierce looked thoughtful.

"Understand Mrs. Hearst is a suffrage sympathizer," McGee said.

"Tell me, McGee," Bierce said, "can you possibly remember the contents of a column from one week to another?"

"I suppose you can't, Mr. Bitter Bierce."

"Especially forgettable are puns," Bierce said, for McGee was a punster.

"So the *Examiner* is going after Will Jaspers as the murderer of Henry Devine."

"Indeed, we are pursuing the murderer of Henry Devine."

"The divine Devine."

"The *Examiner*'s divinity is the truth, McGee."

"Desirability and appearance, you mean, Bierce?"

Truth is a compound of desirability and appearance, as Bierce had defined it in "Prattle."

"In this case truth and a compound of fact and investigation," Bierce said, looking irritated, which pleased McGee, who retracted his probing face like a tortoise.

"I'd as soon pick Devine for murdering Will Jaspers as the opposite," McGee said. He made a saluting gesture with a flattened hand and drifted away among the other drinkers of the Saloon Route.

"What do you suppose he meant by that?" I said.

"I suppose he meant blackmail," Bierce said.

CHAPTER NINE

INCOMPOSSIBLE, adj. Unable to exist if something else exists. Two things are incompossible when the world of being has scope enough for one of them, but not enough for both—as Walt Whitman's poetry and God's mercy to man.

—The Devil's Dictionary

SUNDAY, FEBRUARY 21, 1892

I slid into a pew at the rear of the church. Up front was a small crowd on hand for the early Sunday-morning preaching of the Reverend Stottlemyer. The church was an unpretentious box with raw brick walls, a plain cross on the back wall, and a lectern. The staging for Stottlemyer was a good deal plainer than that of the Reverend Devine. The church smelled of dust and emptiness.

"The Stottle" was a very thin, mop-haired man who must have been six and a half feet in height. He looked rickety in his rusty black suiting, and he moved awkwardly, but his big eyes blazed out at his congregation as he began his sermon. I estimated about thirty people; many gray heads among them, some young men also, but no young women.

"This Monstrous Regiment of Women!" he all but shouted. He did not shake his finger at us so much as hold it out before him like a weapon.

"What are the men thinking of?" he demanded. "To allow their womenfolk to join this monstrous regiment?"

I had two Protestant sermons to compare, Devine's and this one, and this one did not celebrate sin but castigated it, and in fact seemed to define it as anything to do with the feminist movement and suffragism, with that long finger often held up before us. I was grateful for the sermons in Latin at Old St. Mary's, which I could dream through, untouched, if I so desired. This one was not to be dreamed through.

Stottlemyer did love the term "monstrous regiment" and he sang it out frequently, like a chorus.

He strode as he spoke, and he took a short rod from the lectern, with which he smacked the palm of his left hand to emphasize his points.

He spoke of a vigilance committee.

"It will be commanded by responsible men," he said, calmly now. "I will take my place at the forefront. I will appoint the other sane and responsible ministers and vicars and pastors and parsons, all the trustworthy holy men of this city, to form a solid wall of Jesus-men across Market Street, so this monstrous regiment shall not march, but shall flee to their homes and their hotels and their bagnios—yes, bagnios!—where the men in charge of these daughters of Eve will take them to task at last!" Here he gave his hand an especially firm smack.

As I understood the rule of thumb, one might not beat his wife with a rod any bigger around than his thumb, which was about the size of the Reverend Stottlemyer's rod.

There were more threats of action without any specifics as to how an opposition to the parade would actually proceed, and I thought this was mostly blowhard and not a real and present danger. After about ten minutes of fulmination on the Suffragist regiment, Stottlemyer turned to what must be his sermon for the day.

This concerned the Woman at the Well, a Bible story with which I was not familiar. The Samaritan woman had been married five times and was apparently about to marry again when she met Jesus at the well. According to Stottlemyer, the five husbands symbolized her five senses, and the sixth represented false doctrines. I didn't understand this. She recognized Jesus at the well and was converted by the "living water," which somehow symbolized the blood of Jesus, and then, in turn, converted her whole city to Jesus' cause.

Later she voyaged to Rome, where she was martyred after she converted the daughter of Nero and one hundred of her retinue.

"She is named Saint Photine!" Stottlemyer brayed. "And her feast day is March 3, the day the Monstrous Regiment of Women presume to smear with their filth!"

"I say we will celebrate Saint Photine in a different manner!" he proclaimed. He had now calmly settled behind the lectern, so I assumed the sermon was nearly over.

I crossed myself and managed to duck out of the All-Jesus Church before the offertory. I thought no one saw me but the preacher himself.

I was to meet Amanda at the Cyrus Hotel and bring her to Mrs. Atherton's apartment on Nob Hill.

....

Mrs. Atherton's flat was on Jackson Street, up three flights of stone steps with several halts. Amanda's face was bright with perspiration and she swiped at it with a lacy handkerchief from her sleeve. She wore a black-and-blue dress of long vertical lines and a kind of stiff front that concealed any shape of her bosom. The style was called a "cuirass," she told me, smoothing her hands down her front. I gathered that her dress had been recently turned out for her by a fashionable seamstress.

She paused at a landing, puffing a little.

"Oh, my, wouldn't you know Mrs. Atherton would be high up!" she said.

"Wouldn't you know that Mrs. Atherton would devise for us to arrive at a disadvantage!" she said at the next pause in the climb.

Bierce had already arrived—and admitted us with a proprietorial air. Behind him, Mrs. Atherton presented herself in a stately pose, framed and illuminated in a curved doorway of a balcony against the outside daylight, wearing a diaphanous gown of peach-colored silk with voluminous sleeves. She held up a cigarette, puffed at it, and put it down in a saucer on the table, where it lifted an exclamation mark of gray smoke.

"Ah, Tom!" she said. "And this is your cousin, the Suffragist Pearl!"

She advanced, holding out a hand; Amanda took it and curtsied. "It is an honor to meet you, Mrs. Atherton."

"You have quite a glow from my steps, Miss Wilson!"

"We did halt to admire the views."

Bierce said, "Mrs. Atherton's views have the advantage of overseeing the unfortunate parts of the City from the fortunate heights."

"Mr. Bierce disapproves of Nob Hill," Mrs. Atherton explained. "He has accused me of not observing the observances. What does that mean, pray?"

No one answered her. Bierce smirked beneath his moustache.

Her rooms gleamed with fine furniture of red maple, a wide sideboard with an all-encompassing mirror above it, an easy chair, a shiny satin settee. Through a doorway I had a glimpse of a large colored woman in a black dress and white apron.

We were seated on a narrow balcony, Mrs. Atherton with her back to the views of Chinatown and Portsmouth Square, the rest of us arrayed to take advantage of it. We sat on narrow chairs, the table glossily set before us. The maid brought coffee in a fluted silver pot.

Gazing around her, Amanda made attractive sounds of impressed delight. She plucked up one of the rosy peaches the maid had set on the table with a deft snatch of her perfect little hand. Bierce sat militarily straight-backed. I could tell by the slant of his mouth beneath his fair moustache that he was amused at the possibilities of this meeting.

It did not take Mrs. Atherton long to raise the subject that concerned her. "You are a disciple of Mrs. Quinan's, Miss Wilson."

"I am honored to be that, Mrs. Atherton."

"A fine woman! A just cause!"

"Indeed it is!"

"How one searches the female encomium for the barb it must contain," Bierce said.

"Oh, hush, Ambrose," Mrs. Atherton said. "I'm sure we will find those clever words appearing soon in 'Prattle,' " she said, leaning toward Amanda.

"I believe you are one with us, Mrs. Atherton," Amanda said. I admired her deftness with the little knife as she peeled her peach. But I could see from the slight frown that brought her eyebrows together that her concentration was on Mrs. Atherton.

"To some degree, Miss Wilson," Mrs. Atherton said. "I must admit that I have not taken part in organized feminism. There is a certain shrillness, I'm sure you understand. I quote one of my novels: 'If women are dissatisfied with their lives, why don't they change them quietly instead of indulging in parades and polemics?' "

"Yes, I remember reading that," Amanda said, attending to her peach. Her cheeks had reddened.

"And I am concerned about the doctrine of Free Love."

"As I am also," Amanda murmured.

"I understand it is the subject of your preachments. Are you also a varietist?"

"I am that also."

I knew that dreadful word, which was applied to the most extreme of the Free Lovers, with their declared intention of having relations with whomever they wanted whenever they wanted. It was some consolation that Amanda's cheeks were flaming.

Mrs. Atherton looked impressed. "Well, I haven't much regard for the conventions, my dear Miss Wilson, but I must confess I have *some.*"

I was so intent on Amanda's responding to this interrogation respectfully but stoutly that I could feel the ache of my clenched fists. She did not respond at all, and Mrs. Atherton continued: "My great interest has been the independence of women."

"Mine also," Amanda murmured.

"And the female denigrations of motherhood and monotonous domestic routine," Bierce added. "If I have read 'Woman in Her Variety' correctly."

I tried to relax the grip of my fists.

"But not Free Love," Mrs. Atherton said, raising her perfect profile in order to gaze down her nose at Amanda, who looked very small just now, but not cowed.

"My dear, I believe that the ancient commandments against adultery have become such a part of the human spirit that they cannot be ignored without terrible consequences."

"We are surrounded by terrible consequences, which we have managed to ignore for generations!" Amanda said.

"I do confess to an instinct for chastity, Miss Wilson. And I can see no way out of the Material Necessity for women. The Material Necessity cannot be served by Free Love."

I knew enough about the women's movement to know the importance of Material Necessity, which meant the necessity of woman to marry for the essentials of room, board, and a clothing allowance instead of love. I willed Amanda to reply with spirit.

"We must seek a way out of the Material Necessity!" she said, with a determined set to her chin. "Indeed, women must seize the independence you speak of. They must grasp their rights. They must be freed of the Material Necessity by becoming doctors, lawyers, hack drivers, typewriters, editors, and writers—as you are, Mrs. Atherton, who are free of it."

I was proud of her.

"I take it that you are also free of it, if temporarily," Mrs. Atherton said.

"I have a profession. I am a speaker for the Woman's Suffrage Association, and am compensated for my efforts by its subscriptions."

Bierce was smiling, his coffee cup raised almost in a salute.

"It is easy for you and me to disparage the Necessity," Mrs. Atherton said. "But what of the others who are not so fortunate?"

"As you know, Mrs. Atherton, the others you speak of have been deprived of any self possession and ambition by a cruel and unjust system."

"Very well spoken, Miss Wilson!" Bierce said.

"Thank you, Mr. Bierce."

Mrs. Atherton sighed and said, "Ambrose has been castigating marriage since before you were born, Miss Wilson."

" 'A master, a mistress, and two slaves, a total of two,' " I said, quoting Bierce.

Amanda mentioned that she had read Mrs. Atherton's novel *Hermia Suydam* and had been so impressed by it that she had given it to several of her friends to read, who had also been much impressd.

She had found a route to Mrs. Atherton's heart, which set our hostess to purring.

"Whatever gives a true picture of the best of one's own times, a living piece of current history done from firsthand impressions—surely it is of value!"

"*Hermia Suydam* does that!" Amanda said, further impressing Mrs. Atherton with her intelligence. I saw that I had no need to worry about Amanda being able to cope with this situation.

"Of course, Ambrose would say—has said!—that the novel's length works against the aesthetic goal of unity."

The two women gazed at Bierce in sisterly disapproval.

"I have indeed said that," Bierce said, with a bow of his head. "And I am sure that Mrs. Atherton has no doubt that I will say it again." He said to me, "Novelists are collectors of the experiences of others."

"I have had plenty of my own, thank you, Ambrose," Mrs. Atherton said. "It is character that novelists collect.

"Character is so much more important in the novel than the short story," she said triumphantly, just as the maid arrived with plates and serving bowls, an omelet, sizzling bacon, raisin-spotted rolls. The conversation turned to admiration of the breakfast.

But to my distress, Mrs. Atherton returned to the subject of Amanda's morals. "Then you do not contemplate marriage, Miss Wilson?"

Amanda's hand patted mine under the table. "No, I do not, Mrs. Atherton."

"Nor children, then?"

"I suppose I may have a change of heart at some future instance."

My mother would be pleased at such a change of heart.

It was Amanda's turn. "You have been married, I believe, Mrs. Atherton. Did you find it a felicitous experience?"

Bierce touched his handkerchief to his lips to conceal a smile, and Mrs. Atherton also looked amused. "I did not, Miss Wilson, although it fulfilled the Necessity for a time."

And she said, "With the sale of my first novel to *The Argonaut* I was the possessor of the princely sum of one hundred and fifty dollars, with which I proceeded to buy the books I so much desired. My husband castigated me that I had not given him the money to pay the gamblers who were pressing him at that moment."

"And you, Mr. Bierce?"

"There were early felicities. Later my wife was too often in the company of her detestable mother and her doubly detestable brother. We are separated, not divorced."

Bierce called his in-laws the Holy Trinity. Separation from Mrs. Bierce suited him just fine, for it expressed the philosophy of "when falling into a woman's arms, be careful not to fall into her hands." The existence of a Mrs. Bierce kept ambitious females in their place.

Breakfast was consumed, more coffee produced. The main

subject was ignored until Bierce said to Amanda, "Mrs. Atherton has experienced motherhood twice."

"My little boy died several years ago," Mrs. Atherton said. I thought she did not look much grieved.

"There was a girl, also?" Amanda said.

"My Muriel resides with my mother in the City."

"Of course motherhood is the thing for which women were fashioned by their Creator," I said.

Mrs. Atherton looked shocked.

Bierce had asked for a glass of brandy to mix in his coffee, in a manner that convinced me he was very much a familiar here. "That does not sound like you, Tom," he said.

"It is the voice of my mother," I said. "I'm afraid she thinks it is the thing I was fashioned for also—to provide her with a grandchild."

"I understand you are not even married, Tom," Mrs. Atherton said.

"A situation I am hoping to remedy," I said.

Amanda's hand patted mine under the table again. She was sitting with her head high, bright-faced, the lock of fair hair curved over her forehead. I was grateful for the good luck that had made my father's sister's daughter's oldest girl my cousin, and unbelieving in the bad luck that had made her a Free Love varietist, unmoved by proposals of marriage.

"A matter of masters and slaves," Bierce said, pompously.

"What a pretty frock you are wearing, Miss Wilson," Mrs. Atherton said. "I must say, with your pretty face and fine figure, you seem made for the delight of the opposite gender, and not for the very drab and contentious and frequently less-than-lovely company of the other adherents of the feminist cause."

"They are more than lovely in their dedication to that cause, Mrs. Atherton."

Mrs. Atherton's lips compressed in her noble face. She said, "I do understand that your ministerial advocate, the Reverend Devine, was dedicated to Free Love also."

"I am aware of that rumor, Mrs. Atherton," Amanda said. This time her hand touched mine, but did not press.

It was the last contentious exchange. Breakfast stretched out, and the occasion turned into a pleasant one. I thought Amanda had won over Mrs. Atherton and Bierce, as she had won over the male hecklers of her speech at Pierce Hall, as she had won me.

....

When we had departed Mrs. Atherton's breakfast and were heading down Taylor Street, Amanda leaning heavily on my arm as we made our way along the steep sidewalk, she said, "Were you ashamed of me, Cuz?"

"I thought you brilliant."

"That is so nice to hear!"

"Will you marry me?"

"I will most certainly not!"

After a time, when we were on level pavement, she said lightly, "When I first came to the City I thought you had other plans for a relation."

"You are my relation," I said. "I would only have you be a closer one."

"I will not be a married one, Cuz." She released my arm and walked a course at a remove from my side.

I might break my old mother's heart, but I would not trample upon it. "Marriage," I said. "I can only hope will come to seem to you more—felicitous."

"It will not," Amanda said, almost harshly. "And this afternoon I am to come and watch you play baseball. My brothers played baseball."

"I must keep my eye on you," I said.

"And why is that?"

"Because my eye is gratified by the sight."

"That is very nice, Cuz," she said, and took my arm again.

....

The playing fields were in the park on the south side of Market Street. Where the Firemen were scheduled to play the Clampers there was a litle grandstand of four ascending sets of benches. Amanda was seated in the exact center of the rickety structure, in her eye-catching blue dress, with a white parasol shading her.

The Clampers were a burly bunch, wearing sweaters with a sewn-on, yellow ECV on the chest. The right fielder was Frank Patchett, Jaspers's assistant at the Cumberland Bank.

Some games I pitched, some I played catcher. This was a catcher day, with Isaac Deane on the mound. In the second inning Patchett got a base hit, and presently proceeded to third. I should have had an instinct of what was going to happen.

The batter got a hit and was thrown out at first, and Jim Stockwell rocketed the ball to me at home as Patchett charged down the third baseline, the yellow ECV on his sweater enlarging. He didn't slide in, he ran into me full bore. I and the ball were knocked galley west. I lay on the grass, groaning. After Isaac and some other Firemen had picked me up and dusted me off, and had inquired as to my general health, I saw that in the grandstand Amanda was standing with the parasol held up like an inquiry. I waved to her.

Patchett gave me a snarl of a grin: "Sorry, Redmond."

"That's all right," I said, with my teammates standing around looking worried. It was all right, all right.

We were up 6–2 in the fifth inning when it began to set up again, Patchett with a hit the shortstop fumbled, Patchett on second, and then on third, grinning down the line at me. Then he was coming at me out of the afternoon sun like a locomotive.

This time I stepped aside and smacked mitt and ball into his groin as he banged past me. He screamed. The collision sent me spinning like a turnstile, but I was still on my feet, whereas he was tagged out and writhing on the ground. With a shout the Clampers on the bench rose like bears to surround me, and the Firemen sprinted in from the field for my protection. A shouting match ensued then, with Patchett helped up, white-faced and clutching his crotch. Amanda was on her feet in the grandstand again.

"Sorry, Patchett," I called out to calm things down, which satisfied some. But there were still Clampers who seemed to want my scalp—especially the first baseman, whose rank language it was difficult not to respond to. The Clampers had no one to replace Patchett so the game was called. Patchett was dragged groaning off with two infielders supporting him. He turned one black glance back to warn me that this was not the end of it.

....

"I didn't see what happened," my pretty cousin said when she and I started away from the field together, my mitt and some balls and bats in a canvas bag slung over my shoulder. "All those other people seemed angry at you."

"Just so you weren't ashamed of me," I said.

"I thought you were brilliant, Cuz!" she said, laughing and latching on to my free arm.

CHAPTER TEN

INCUMBENT, n. A person of the liveliest interest to the outcumbents.
— *The Devil's Dictionary*

MONDAY, FEBRUARY 22, 1892

When I looked into Bierce's office, Mrs. Atherton stood behind Bierce at his desk, bending forward to gaze at typewritten pages before him on the desktop. He waved me to a seat.

The sun through the window haloed Mrs. Atherton's pile of hair with gold.

"What you have here," Bierce was saying to her, "is 'Is she really dead?' she said.' The 'dead' and 'said' make an unfortunate rhyme, so this may be one of the few places where you may employ a different speech verb than 'said.' 'Whispered,' however, will not do as the line of dialog contains no *ess*es, which are a fundamental of whispering."

"Goodness!" Mrs. Atherton said, straightening to present me with a chilly smile. "Isn't Ambrose a fine-toothed editor, Tom!"

I agreed with her.

Bierce continued: "Let us consider the line of dialog itself. 'Is she really dead?' Death is dire. The word 'really' seems lightsome rather than dire. Is she 'surely' dead? 'Surely,' you see, has a long vowel sound, 'really' a short one. A long vowel sound gives a more dire implication, but 'Is she surely dead?' seems awkward. Let us try, 'Are you *sure* she's dead?' "

"I'm not at the moment *sure* of anything!" Mrs. Atherton said, standing before the window with her hands to her head as though holding it on. "What have you done to my poor line of dialog, Ambrose?"

"I suggest you follow the same guideline in the names of characters," Bierce went on. He grinned at me under his moustache. "Your heroine here is named Vinnie. I believe the course of her life is to be a tragic one. I suggest a name containing a long vowel sound—long vowel sounds for the names of principal characters, shorter vowel sounds for the names of lesser characters."

"You will say next that the same principle holds for titles," Mrs. Atherton said.

"The title, *Silver Circles*, would consequently be found wanting," Bierce said nodding. "A perfect title is *Murders in the Rue Morgue*. So many long vowels, such implications of villainy and doom. Indeed, I commend 'doom' as a splendid, titular word.

"May I keep this a little longer?" He indicated the pile of manuscript on his desk.

"Indeed you may!" Mrs. Atherton said with a sigh.

....

When she had left us, he said to me, "The route to a woman's heart lies through her manuscript."

Indeed, it was the route Amanda had found to lead to Mrs. Atherton's heart yesterday.

"Some manuscripts are quite beyond help," Bierce said. He was known to help pretty young poetesses with their lines, whose authors and whose genre he as often scarified in "Prattle."

"Mrs. Atherton's?"

"She is talented. I can help her when her prose becomes lazy and hurried, for she is in a hurry! She is very good on plot and character, but you know my opinion on the novel as a literary form."

"And hers on the short story."

He uttered a mirthless laugh.

I knew he wore his heart on his sleeve, for all his bitter disparagement of the feminine gender. I thought Mrs. Atherton might fancy him herself, but as I considered the road ahead of them I could not come up with an ending that was not best expressed in long vowel sounds.

TUESDAY, FEBRUARY 23, 1892

BANKER MURDERED

WILLIAM P. JASPERS SHOT DEAD

HIS WIFE FOUND THE BODY

The Examiner *will investigate*

Bierce and I stood with Captain Chandler and a detective in uniform in the Bull Clamper's study in his medium-sized but quite tall mansion on Taylor Street on the flank of Nob Hill. This was a mahogany-walled room with windows looking south over the Tenderloin, and a high shelf surrounding the room on which were set trophies and mementos in their hundreds, waiting for the next earthquake to knock them to the floor. A bookcase solid with red- and blue-bound sets of books occupied the north wall, behind the desk.

Jaspers had been seated at his desk when the assassin shot him in the heart. Entry had been through a cellar window, and presumably up the back stairs.

Captain Chandler looked discouraged, his cap under his arm. Bierce stood gazing at the display of objects on the shelf as though they were a challenge to his deductive powers.

"Wife didn't hear any shot," Chandler said. "She was somewhere downstairs in this big house, and it could've been any time last evening."

"Did you discuss the Reverend Devine with her?"

"Didn't do that yet." Chandler scraped his fingers through his chin whiskers reflectively.

"Vice president of the Cumberland Bank," I said. "I suppose a banker has enemies."

Chandler said in a tired voice, "Jaspers was in charge of the till. The president's old Garrett Stevens. He don't have the wits anymore to attend to business."

Bierce reached up for a silver figure of a large-busted, scantily clothed lady, inscribed: E CLAMPUS VITAS, ESPECIALLY WIDDERS.

"It is the Clamper motto," Bierce told Chandler. "Widders and orphins, especially widders."

Chandler produced a wintry smile.

"He was the Noble Grand Humbug of the San Francisco Chapter, which is like the chairman. He was sworn to interfere with the Suffrage Parade. Devine supported it. What do you make of that?"

Chandler shook his head. The detective had taken the cue from Bierce and was prowling the room, squinting up at the objects displayed on the shelf. There were statuettes; a painted toy horse; rocks showing mineral; cups, plates, and saucers adorned with inscribed words celebrating various expositions and gatherings.

Bierce replaced the silver widow and went to inspect the desk. On the broad oak surface was a photograph of a pretty woman in a broad hat, holding her gloves before her like a dead rabbit. Bierce picked it up and inspected the lady, who must be the present Mrs. Jaspers.

"Summon Mrs. Jaspers, if you please," he said to the detective, who looked to Chandler for confirmation, received it, and departed.

Mrs. Jaspers arrived promptly, a slim figure in black, her head covered in a black veil so that there was only a sense of dark eyes, a pale forehead, and cheeks.

"You discovered your husband's body, Mrs. Jaspers?"

"Yes," she whispered.

"I am very sorry for your tragedy, madame, but I must demand that we be shown the pearls that the Reverend Devine gave you. Will you bring them to us?"

She seemed to vibrate beneath the black netting. Without a word she turned and left the room. She returned moments later and extended to Bierce an ornately carved ivory box. He opened the lid to reveal the stock of pearls inside.

"Thank you, Mrs. Jaspers. He showed the open box to Chandler, to the detective, and to me.

"What does it mean, Mr. Bierce?" Chandler said.

"I promise you that I will find out what it means."

He swung toward the black-clad woman again, who said, "Will I have those back, Mr. Bierce? They are precious to me."

"They will be safe with Captain Chandler, Mrs. Jaspers. That will be all. Thank you for your cooperation."

She swept out of the study, past the detective, who looked puzzled. Bierce handed the box of pearls to the chief of detectives.

"Captain Chandler," he said. "It may be construed that

each of these pearls symbolizes an infidelity. In the case of the Reverend Devine, there are a great many women with vengeful husbands to be investigated. In this case there is no doubt a host of suspects who have been denied loans or have otherwise been offended by the authority and arrogance of Mr. Jaspers as a bank vice president. But the two cases seem to me to be connected by the two pearls in the decorated cup and this box of pearls.

"Furthermore, there may be a connection to the Suffrage Parade through one or more of the suffrage Pearls, even though Mr. Jaspers was on one side of the matter and the Reverend Devine on the other.

"And there is also a principle I have always found of the utmost importance," he went on. "Why *now*? The Suffrage Parade is a week away. Two days ago Jaspers was exposed in the *Examiner* as the murderer Edwards—who shot his wife's seducer—and the vengeful husband responsible for the tragedy his wife's life became."

"Ah!" Chandler said.

"Jaspers's first wife must have had a son by him. Or by the lover Larrikin."

Chandler was nodding. "You are a clever man, Mr. Bierce. I expect that chap will be the man we are looking for." He held up the ivory box. "There do seem to be pearls everywhere. And there is a tip I have had of the three Pearl ladies in danger."

"What are you doing about that, Captain?"

"I have set a patrolman at their hotel to watch out for trouble." Chandler tweaked his whiskers anxiously.

"What of the ladies who waited on the Reverend Devine?"

"Those are devoted ladies. Every one."

"I must speak to them," Bierce said unhappily.

....

Later Bierce found a low stepladder and moved it around the edges of the room, climbing to the high step and examining the clutter of objects on the ledge. He brought down and set on the desk several items, one a brass cup with the engraved words COLFAX CHORAL SOCIETY 1888. Another was a red pottery horse, carrying the word ZANTA, a third a little cheap metal model of a two-story house, with a painted sign whose message was half worn off but still legible: HOOLIGAN HOUSE, COLFAX.

"Colfax," I said, when he had folded his ladder and leaned it against the wall.

"Are you familiar with Colfax, Tom?"

I was. Colfax, named for U. S. Grant's vice president, was about fifty miles east of Sacramento on the Central Pacific Railroad line.

I saw that a trip there might be in order for me.

CHAPTER ELEVEN

ACQUAINTANCE, n. A person whom we know well enough to borrow from, but not well enough to lend to.

—The Devil's Dictionary

TUESDAY, FEBRUARY 23, 1892

The old banker Garrett Stevens was seated at Jaspers's desk when I was ushered in, and remained so. He had a face fantastically wrinkled and liver-spotted, and perhaps twenty strands of gray hair combed straight across his shiny bald head. An ear trumpet stood flared end down on his desk. He scowled ferociously at the mention of Frank Patchett's name.

"Fired him!" he said. "Fired him this morning. Didn't like him at first. Don't like him now. Never will like him. Sent him packing. How else can I help you, Mr. Redmond?" He propped the ear trumpet to his ear.

"Fired him why?"

"Didn't like him. Didn't I make that clear?"

"He was Jaspers's cashier."

"Not mine, sir! Irregularities? Maybe, maybe not! Fellow acted as though he was the Angel Gabriel, prancing around the premises."

"Jaspers had employed him?"

After some adjustment of his trumpet Stevens understood

this. "Fellow came from St. Louis. I will tell you it seems to me there were irregularities going on. Why did Will hire this fellow? Something underhanded, I believe. Now, how else can I help you, Mr. Redmond? I have a meeting in"—after consulting his watch, faceup on his desk—"eight minutes!"

"Do you think there was some pressure on Mr. Jaspers to hire him?"

"Didn't say that!" the old man said.

He picked up his watch and shook it. "Seven minutes."

"I am investigating Jaspers's murder," I said.

Stevens straightened in his chair as though he had been jerked by a rope. His wrinkled and spotted face seemed to collapse in upon itself.

"Are you now? Well, then this conversation is terminated! Good day, sir!"

....

With Bierce, in his office, was a Mr. James Carling, a glass-of-fashion gent of about sixty with a violet in his buttonhole, high collar, ruby ring on his left pinkie, and a neat graying growth of whiskers.

"Mr. Carling is the chairman of the board of directors of the God Is Love Church on Clay Street," Bierce informed me, after introductions. "He points out that the church was not the property of the Reverend Devine, but of the board of directors."

I asked if they had appointed a new minister.

"Mr. Blaisedell from Palo Alto will address us this Sunday. Negotiations are in progress."

Bierce said, "I imagine there will be deliberations of a moral nature."

Carling's cheeks reddened. "Mr. Bierce, you have promised me that none of our conversation will appear in 'Prattle.' "

"That is my promise," Bierce said. He said to me, "Mr. Carling is well aware of the Reverend Devine's reputation."

"So is everyone," I said, thinking of Amanda.

"And Mrs. Carling?" Bierce inquired.

"I suspect you will find this ridiculous, Mr. Bierce, but I have one kind of relation with Clara, while Henry Devine had another. My wife has both a higher and a lower nature, and Henry appealed to the higher with my full confidence."

Bierce maintained a perfectly straight face. "With your full confidence, you say, sir?"

"I do indeed."

"Such confidence is very rare."

"I am aware of that, sir!"

Carling's confidence might be very rare, but there was clearly a heightening of blood in his cheeks.

"Mr. Carling," Bierce said, "I must ask if you have been the victim of blackmail in the matter of your wife and Henry Devine."

Carling's cheeks turned from red to pale in an instant. He gazed at Bierce with lips compressed to a scar.

"Yes, I have," he said.

"The blackmailer was William Jaspers?"

Carling's eyes bugged. "Yes, it was."

"And you paid?"

"I did not shoot Will Jaspers, Mr. Bierce."

"How many times had he demanded payment?"

"Just once."

"And the sum?"

"Five hundred dollars."

"Was that to be the end of it?"

"So he said."

Bierce said, "Can you tell me how the demand for blackmail was conveyed to you, Mr. Carling?"

"We were thrown together at the bar at the Pacific Club, where he acted as though he had just remembered something. 'Oh, by the way, James—' sort of thing. He was quite insouciant. I said, 'But this is blackmail, Will!' and he laughed and said, 'Of course it is. You must watch Mrs. Carling more carefully.' Such a thing had never happened to me before, and the sum was not such that I felt obliged to take other steps. He sent his assistant to collect, very businesslike.

"I didn't kill him, Mr. Bierce. Such a thing is foreign to my nature."

"It may be that William Jaspers engaged in blackmail with someone to whose nature it was not foreign."

"Frank Patchett was the collector," I said.

"Yes, he was. He acted as if it were quite an ordinary transaction, as though he were merely collecting on a note for the bank."

"Cash?" I asked.

"Cash was stipulated."

I said, "Is Frank Patchett a member of your congregation, Mr. Carling?"

There was more reaction in his wooden features than I would have expected. He looked me full in the face, nodding.

"And what is your interest in Mr. Patchett, Mr. Redmond?"

"I've just come from the Cumberland Bank, where Mr. Stevens has fired him."

"It is naturally interesting to us that he was a participant in this blackmail," Bierce said.

"*My* interest is in the Suffragist ladies, one of whom is a relative," I said. "William Jaspers threatened to employ the Clampers to savage their parade, and Patchett seemed to be his strong right arm."

Bierce's desk skull regarded me vacantly.

"It is difficult for me to believe that Frank Patchett was connected with blackmail," Carling said. "I would venture to say that he was not aware of the illegality of his mission. He did seem to emulate Jaspers, cut his whiskers the same way, as though he was trying to look like his mentor."

"Patchett has the sound of an assumed name," Bierce said.

"That is common enough in San Francisco," Carling said, and now seemed more at ease.

"When did the encounter with Jaspers at the Pacific Club take place?" Bierce wanted to know.

"About two weeks before the murder of Henry Devine."

I had a sense that Carling no longer felt himself threatened by this line of questioning, and Bierce must have sensed the same, for he thanked the chairman of the board of directors of the God Is Love Church, and dismissed him.

....

"I had some difficulty with the concept of his wife's two natures," I said, when Carling had left us.

"So much so that I wonder if he was pulling our leg," Bierce said.

"I don't think leg-pulling is part of his nature."

"He is an attorney of considerable reputation and rectitude—as you no doubt noticed. Are we to believe your baseball opponent Patchett is a blackmailer?"

"That may be how he got his job at the Cumberland Bank. Jaspers's secrets."

"We will see what Mammy has been able to uncover. Now we must call upon Mr. Borden Chase."

....

The Chase mansion was on the western slope of Nob Hill, not far from the Jaspers mansion. We met Borden Chase in a large room with high windows paneled in redwood that glowed with wax. He was a bespectacled, balding man of medium height who gave each of us a smart jerk of a handshake before indicating upholstered chairs.

"I take it that this is an interview of some importance, Mr. Bierce."

Seated, legs crossed, Bierce said, "I have information that your wife had a particular relation with the Reverend Devine."

Chase blinked but otherwise seemed unaffected. "You should speak with Mrs. Chase about that." He reached for a bell rope.

"One moment, Mr. Chase," Bierce said. "I must ask if you have been approached by a blackmailer."

"I have not, sir. Again I must refer you to Mrs. Chase, who controls her own funds."

A butler was summoned, who summoned Mrs. Chase. Mr. Chase departed upon her arrival. She was a small woman, all in black, whose black slippers whispered on the parquet as she approached us. She was much younger than her husband, with a small, piquant face and large eyes. She shook hands as though she were learning something in the process.

Seated again, Bierce said, "I have information that you had a particular relation with the Reverend Henry Devine."

She inclined her sleek head until her face was hidden from us. "Must I answer that?"

"I am investigating the murders of Henry Devine and William Jaspers, Mrs. Chase. I hope that some information you may be able to furnish will be helpful to that cause."

"And will that information be confidential, Mr. Bierce?"

"Insofar as I can control it, madame."

"The answer, then, is yes. I was quite in love with Henry Devine, Mr. Bierce. I am fully aware that I was only one of several."

"And were you approached by a blackmailer?"

She inclined her head so her face was hidden again, as though she would ask again if she must answer that. But she said, "I was."

"Were you aware of the identity of the blackmailer?"

She shook her head. "The transaction was conducted entirely by mail."

"And the sum?"

"The sum was six hundred dollars."

"Was that to be the end of it?"

"Yes it was. And has been."

It occurred to me that Mrs. Chase wore black for Henry Devine.

I said, "I am acquainted with a young woman who thought she was in love with the Reverend Devine. She told me that she had discovered that he was not so beautiful on the inside as he was on the outside."

She stared at me with her little teeth clenched. Her eyes seemed to spark and yet not focus on me. It was clear to me that she was mad.

She said, "I will hear no abuse of that saintly man! He was beautiful in his entirety!"

"Women have certainly thought so," I said, retreating.

"Indeed they have! It was like being wrapped in a holy cloak! It was like being wrapped in angel wings. It was like being transported—" She stopped, moving her head from side to side as though the collar of her dress was too tight.

Bierce was leaning back in his chair with his lips puffed out helplessly.

"Men cannot understand, of course," Mrs. Chase concluded, straightening.

"Yet Mr. Chase understands?" Bierce said.

"He does!" *Meaning,* I thought, *He'd better!*

When we had finished our interview with Mrs. Chase and

were accompanied to the door by the butler, I saw, across the room, Mr. Chase peeking through a half-opened door there.

....

"Kansas," Mammy said, seated beside Bierce's desk, her thin, hard face pressed toward him like a dark blade. "Kansas!" she said. "Quantrill! William Jaspers had a different name then, but he was with Quantrill when the Confederates destroyed Lawrence."

She leaned back, as though to let this sink in. Bloody Kansas. Mammy had been a supporter of John Brown, who had murdered Confederate settlers at Potawatomie Creek. In the horrific Lawrence Raid, Quantrill's guerrilla army had raped, pillaged, and murdered antislavery inhabitants. John Brown in the fifties, Quantrill in sixty-three, thirty years ago. Jaspers must have been in his late fifties, early sixties. A young man in Kansas during the War, when anger ran high and murder hung on pro or anti.

"Name of Edward Sayles," Mammy said. "Gunman for Quantrill. One of the Lawrence killers. That was a devilish bad bunch of men, those Confederates that rousted Lawrence. There'd've been a price on Sayles's head. There'd been warrants after the war, too."

"So he came on West," Bierce said, leaning back with his hands steepled. "I would question Frank Patchett as an assumed name. I wonder if his patronymic is not Sayles."

Mammy stared in a silence, like a curtain lowered. "I can find that out," she said.

When she had gone, I said, "Do you think this is the track of Jaspers's killer?"

"It is a track we must explore," Bierce said. "And the next stop is Colfax."

"I'll take the morning train," I said.

....

Again my first impression upon entering the hotel room was that the Trey of Pearls was practicing Living Statues. Amanda perched on the arm of a sofa with her hands raised in greeting; Bird Girl was supported supine on a long table behind the sofa; and Emmiline Prout stood on her tiptoes, facing me, with an arm out for balance. Mrs. Quinan sat in a rocking chair, holding a big book, no doubt *War and Peace*.

I stood gazing around at them, holding my hat in my two hands.

Mrs. Quinan closed the book with a clap. "It is our friend Mr. Redmond!" she said.

Amanda tripped over to kiss me on the cheek, eliciting smiles from Emmiline and Gloria.

"You are aware there is a patrolman outside in the hall," I said.

"We have met Mr. Peterson," Mrs. Quinan said. Her pince-nez glasses gave her an expression of having a headache. She removed them, squinting at me.

"Then you know there is a threat of danger."

"That is very exciting, Cuz!"

"No, it is not," I said. "You must be careful of your movements."

"Oh, we are, Mr. Redmond!" Bird Girl chirped, switching around on her table so she was seated facing me.

"What kind of danger?" Emmiline wanted to know. Her dark hair was pulled back severely from her pale face. All three of them wore their uniform white dresses with the narrow black belts; Mrs. Quinan wore purple changeable silk with a tent of a bosom, her graying hair in a stack.

"It is E Clampus Vitas, is it not?" Mrs. Quinan said.

"There's also that crazy preacher."

"Mr. Jaspers has been murdered!" Emmiline said. She seated herself on the sofa with a graceful sweep of her skirt. Amanda stood a little too close to me, gazing into my eyes.

"We have been warned, Cuz!" she said. "That man you collided with at baseball yesterday."

"Patchett?"

"He spoke of Mr. Jaspers's position in E Clampus Vitas, and maintained that it would still prevail."

"He was Jaspers's assistant at the bank."

"He told us we must not try to march," Mrs. Quinan said. "I said on the contrary, we would very much try to march. He was quite rude! Amanda says you and he had an encounter on the baseball field."

"Ladies—" I started.

"Cuz, if you are going to say we must not march because it is dangerous, I tell you that we *will* march!"

"I only want you to be careful," I said. "I have to go out of town."

"Who murdered Mr. Jaspers, Mr. Redmond?" Emmiline inquired. "Surely it cannot be the same person who shot poor Henry Devine. And *why*?"

"I believe Mr. Patchett thought we had to do with it!" Gloria Robinson said. She emitted a cackle, which went on too long, until Mrs. Quinan said, "Gloria!" halting her.

I said, "Mr. Bierce believes he was murdered because of something in the piece about him in the *Examiner* concerning the murder twenty years ago."

"And must you leave town to solve it, Cuz?"

"I'll take the train in the morning. I have told Peterson I'll have his liver if anything happens to you."

"We are certainly not going to remain cooped in this hotel room because of some rumor!" Emmiline Prout said, with a flounce.

"I want the three of you to stay together, and Peterson to accompany you if you go out."

"I believe you have our best interests at heart, Mr. Redmond," Mrs. Quinan said.

"After all, my cousin is one of you."

There was silence at that. Bird Girl gazed at me with her otherworldly eyes as though seeing me for the first time.

"Is a cousin variety, Mandy?" she said to Amanda.

Amanda colored. I saw from Mrs. Quinan's expression that Bird Girl was a constant irritant to her.

I was invited to seat myself between Amanda and Emmiline, with Gloria still perched on the table behind us, and Mrs. Quinan opposite. I could feel Amanda's thigh against mine.

"Mr. Patchett does resemble Mr. Jaspers," Mrs. Quinan said, still holding the thick volume on her lap.

"I have heard it said that drinkingmen eventually come to resemble each other," Emmiline said, which must be the W.C.T.U. sentiment that Jaspers had decried.

"Mrs. Hearst has given us a thousand dollars toward the cause, Cuz!" Amanda said. "Is that not generous?"

"What of Willie Hearst?" I asked. "Can he be called a friend?"

"The *Examiner* has not been *un*friendly," Mrs. Quinan said.

"That is because of Cousin Tom!" Amanda said.

Mrs. Quinan scowled at her. "My dear, I would be more comfortable if you and Mr. Redmond were not quite so snugly squeezed together on the sofa."

Emmiline instantly flounced to one side to give us more room.

"Amanda does like to be snugly squeezed with gentlemen," Bird Girl said.

"Gloria!"

Amanda tensed her leg against mine, and then shifted a few inches away. She was laughing.

When I left she accompanied me to the door, but there were no kisses. "Come back to me," she whispered.

I promised that I would.

CHAPTER TWELVE

SELF-EVIDENT, adj. Evident to one's self and to nobody else.
— The Devil's Dictionary

WEDNESDAY, FEBRUARY 24, 1892

From my car on the Union Pacific I could see the long green canyons slanting up to the distant ridges of the Sierra Nevada, where peaks were streaked with snow. I disembarked at the cupolaed station in Colfax, across the street from a stretch of boardwalk and a row of false-fronted buildings. The air was sun warmed, with a tinge of chill to it, and a sweet redolence of pines.

My father had recommended the pharmacist, Grady Boggs. In the pharmacy he stood behind a counter, before racks of pale, milky ceramic bottles, their contents marked in fancy script. He was a lanky, moustached fellow in gartered shirtsleeves and a striped apron.

"So you are Clete Redmond's boy," he said, presenting me with a pale hand to shake.

"My visit here has to do with Dora McCall," I told him.

"Surely, I knew Dora," he said. "She was Dora Morton when she come back up here. Died up at the sanitarium." He waved a hand.

Against my protestations he locked up the pharmacy to

guide me on a stroll through the town. He pointed out a small gray house perched on a hillside, where the McCalls had lived when Dora was a girl, and where her aged mother still eked out a long illness. On the opposite hillside the Presbyterian Church raised a steeple like a monitory finger. There Dora McCall had sung in the choir.

"I wonder where she would have met her first husband," I said.

"That Edwards fellow. Well, she went down to Sacramento with a church group, met him there as I heard it. Run off with him. She was just a bit of a thing, sixteen, seventeen I think. He's the one shot the Englisher."

"He's the one," I said. "He divorced her."

"That's right. She was surely the victim of that mess down there. Ruined her life, it surely did."

"There was a son," I said.

"Son by Morton," he said, nodding. "Took Morton's name anyhow. Morton was a gambler fellow. Dora surely did have poor luck in her husbands."

"Where is young Morton now?"

"Left out of here a couple of years ago. I don't know where he went."

"How old would he be?"

"About like his mother was when she left—sixteen, seventeen. Maybe he's nineteen now. Slip of a fellow, like her. Sang up at the church, like her.

"Sad little fellow," he went on. "That's a poor thing for a boy, his mother dying like that. Loved his mother, devoted to her. Took ill himself when she died. I know; I furnished him laudanum and such for his weeping. Grandmother's a crotchety sort. Mrs. Fairchild. She is bed-bound now, nurse living in. There will be money due him from the sale of the house when she passes on. You might tell Bobby that if you run into him. I hope he found a better life down below than he had here."

When we had returned to the pharmacy I excused myself for a walk alone, and directed my steps up the stone-cobbled path to the church. In the dim interior regular gleams of light reflected off the curved backs of the pews, leading up to a platform and a lectern, and a suspended golden cross. I seated myself in the last pew of a third protestant church and tried to beam my thoughts to Bobby Morton.

A fat man tromped in and seated himself beside me; I guessed he was the minister from his backward collar. He introduced himself.

"Stranger in town," he said in a deep voice.

I told him I was trying to find out what I could about Robert Morton.

"Sang in my choir. Had a fine voice," the minister said. "It never changed on him."

"What was he like?"

"Well, he didn't make much of an impression. You know his mother died up in the sanitarium. Other boys made fun of him. I put on a Christmas pageant one year, and he was an angel. Put a lot into it, too. Too much. Wings and a blond wig and rouge on his face. Other boys never let him forget it—called him Angie, and Saint Annie, things like that. I understood he went down to Sacramento and into service to some rich family down there."

"Who would know?" I asked.

"You might talk to Grady Boggs at the pharmacy. He is Mister Know-All of Colfax."

I'd already talked to Grady Boggs, and I jacked up my courage and crossed over to the other hillside to call on Robert Morton's grandmother.

An Indian nurse with a mashed brown face let me in.

A bed had been set up in the parlor, and the woman I assumed to be Mrs. Fairchild, mother of Dora McCall, grandmother of Robert Morton, lay in it, propped up by pillows, a gray, square, old face surrounded by a tangle of gray hair. Eyes swam at me through thick spectacles.

"It is the pastor!" Her eyes blinked at me.

I started to say, "I'm not—"

The Indian nurse pushed me toward the chair beside the bed.

"I thought you would never come, Mr. Pettigrew!" Mrs. Fairchild cried.

"I'm not—"

When I was seated beside the bed she seized my hand with a grip of iron. "I have waited so long! Tell me one of your stories of faith, Mr. Pettigrew!"

"I'm—"

"Oh, Mr. Pettigrew! I have waited and waited! *Please!*" Her hand gripped mine.

"The Woman at the Well," I said.

"Ah, yes! Her grip subsided a bit.

"She recognized Jesus, this Samaritan woman. He confided in her that he was the Son of God."

"Ah, yes, Pastor!"

"Married five times," I said. "The five senses, you see. And the sixth, the false doctrines!"

"I don't understand that, Mr. Pettigrew!"

"Have faith, Mrs. Fairchild! This woman took her faith from the living water, and converted the entire town to Jesus!"

"Ah!"

"And went to Rome where she was martyred, and became

Saint Photine. Before they martyred her she had converted Nero's daughter and a hundred others!"

"What a comfort you are, Mr. Pettigrew!"

"Trust in Jesus!" I said.

"Yes, yes!"

"Your grandson," I said.

"Robert!"

"He was William Jaspers's son?"

"Oh, yes, Will's! Yes. He took that terrible Morton man's name, you see."

"Where is he?"

"Ah, Pastor, I wish I knew. That bad boy, not to let his loving grandmother know—"

She snored.

I squeezed her hand.

She said, "Working at the grandest mansion in Sacramento, he said. Taking care of a—menagerie! A march of bears, something like that. *Osos,* that's Mexican for bears!" She snored.

"Where is he now?"

"Ah, I don't know that, Pastor," she said sleepily. "Caring for a march of osos—at Sacramento. In a grand mansion! Such a beautiful voice, Robert had. And my Dora! We—" She snored again.

That was the end of it. The Indian woman touched my shoulder and made sleeping gestures. Mrs. Fairchild's head had slumped forward, and the nurse plucked the spectacles from her nose, and indicated the door.

....

From the window of my car on the westbound out of Colfax, I gazed at the church where Robert Morton had sung in the choir, and at the hillside house where he had lived with his grandmother, and at the storefronts of Main Street Colfax, and wondered what I was missing and worried that concern for Amanda had caused me to abandon my research in Colfax too soon.

As the locomotive chuffed and the cars picked up speed, a little and a little more, I glanced out my window, into the countenance of a burly fellow standing on the platform in a black suit and derby hat.

It was Frank Patchett, with his chin beard like William Jaspers's beard, and his tugboat jaw. He gazed at me blankly, and I felt my own face stiffen into a reflection of his face.

He was too old to be Robert Morton!

....

In my parents' house in Sacramento there was still the slightest sniff of mud from the years the Sacramento River had flooded the lower-lying parts of town. My mother embraced me, gray hair parted precisely down the middle of her head, smelling of cachet, her tired but still-pretty face marred by the raccoon patches of dark flesh beneath her eyes. She wore a blue housedress and the furry slippers I had given her for her birthday.

"Tommy, Tommy!" she said.

"Where's the gent?"

"He'll be home any minute now!"

Gripping my arm, she led me into the parlor, with its familiar pink settee and my father's fake leather chair, a pull-down lamp, net curtains on the window, and a stack of newspapers beside the chair.

"Oh, I do so worry that you are not eating properly," my mother said.

"I frequent the second-rate fine restaurants of San Francisco looking for the food my mother used to make!"

"Oh, Tommy! But you do look well!"

I thought I would not bring up the subject of being in love until my father was on hand as ballast. "You, too!" I said.

"How are your bowels, Tommy? Are you being regular?"

"All fine in that department."

"I've got new teeth. Aren't they pretty?" She bared her teeth at me.

"*You*'re pretty."

"Your father has a kidney stone. Isn't that a shame? It's not a very big one."

"Poor fellow!"

And thank God the gent arrived just then, with some scuffling and boot whacking on the front porch, and the door banging against its stop. He had always arrived at home like a hurricane coming ashore.

"Tommy!"

So we were seated, my father in his chair, my mother and I flank to flank on the settee.

I explained my mission to Colfax and the Jaspers murder case, the present and the past, of which my father, of course, knew much more than I.

"The grandest mansion in Sacramento!" he said. "That'd be Governor Beal's place, surely. I don't know about a menagerie. A march of bears? *Osos?*" He jacked his eyebrows up and down, looking thoughtful.

"What's a march of bears?"

My father shook his head. "There used to be bull- and bear fights. Haven't heard of one for years."

"Who's Governor Beal?"

"He was one of the Big Four bunch. The mansion's over on N Street. It *is* plenty grand."

"Robert Morton's mother died in the sanitarium up near Colfax."

"Father was a no-good gambler, Benny Morton. He's dead, too, as I told you. Alcohol."

Here my mother became confused and I told her that Robert Morton's mother had been married and divorced by William Jaspers, who had shot her lover twenty years ago. Married a gambler named Morton, and died in a tuberculosis sanitarium in the foothills. I was looking for the son in connection with the murder. When I had first set out it had seemed a frail connection, but it had taken on some muscle when I had glimpsed Frank Patchett on the station platform in Colfax.

I said, "There's a preacher in San Francisco who may have come from Stockton, who may have been run out of town for some peculation. He might be of importance to this investigation. Name of Stottlemyer now. Very tall, maybe six feet six, skinny, mop of black hair. If you know anybody in Stockton—"

Of course my father did. "I'll be in touch," he said.

My mother said, coyly, "And when am I going to have a sweet little grandchild to cuddle, Tommy?"

My father and I frowned at each other.

"I have a proposal on the table," I said.

"And who is it, dear? I hope she is a good Catholic girl."

I shook my head. I couldn't even truthfully stipulate that Amanda was "good." "She's a cousin."

My father cleared his throat. "She's Lolly's oldest girl, hon."

"Oh! Oh, well, she always was a pretty little thing. Except for the freckles. And a little snippy with her parents, I always thought."

I'd never seen that freckled, snippy child, had never even been to Denver.

"But how old could she be, Cletus?"

"Old enough," the gent said. "She's a Suffragist. She's one of those speaker-girls. She gives talks in halls on women's suffrage."

"But she must be eight years younger than Tommy! And a second cousin!"

"Old enough," I said. I was feeling the familiar oppression that I knew my father, also, was aware of, and tried to mitigate. "Old enough and a *second* cousin," I said. "I love her."

"Amanda Jane was always very affectionate," my mother said. "But snippy, I thought."

"Well, she's a Suffragist preacher," I said. "You'd be proud of her if you heard her go at it."

"I am all for women's suffrage, Tommy!"

My father looked so worried I could feel the oppression lifting a little.

My mother said, "But some of those young women are very *wild*!"

"Well," I said. "They are up against some male villainy. They are having a parade next week in the City, and some E Clampus Vitas brutes are sworn to disrupt it."

"Oh, that's terrible!" my mother said. My father's expression of anxiety continued to relieve me.

"Men can certainly act like brutes," my mother went on, forcefully. "And of course there are always women who will toady to them. You know, when I was a young woman we were told that we were not supposed to have any feelings of *that* kind at all. Not at all! Proper young women must be 'passionless.' That is so ridiculous. If you had any feelings of *that* kind you were abnormal! Women were just not supposed to have the 'amative impulse.' That's what they called it!"

My father laid his hand perpendicular to the corner of his mouth and said to me, "Ho! Ho!"

I did not think my mother's protestations were radical enough to mention Amanda's profession of Free Love.

She said, "But some of these women are too noisy to suit me. You know, Tommy, when the people who are leading get too far out in front of the people who want to follow—well, they just lose touch!"

I was afraid Amanda Jane was far out in front.

"Tommy, some of those women have turned against having babies! Amanda Jane is not like that, is she?"

"She is perfect, in my estimation," I said. "I just have to change her mind about marrying me, that's all."

Her eyes searched my face fearfully.

"Don't you worry," I said. "I'll get you a baby yet."

"I do wish you'd hurry, dear! I'm not getting any younger."

"Yes, she is, isn't she, Pa?"

"Indeed she is!" the gent said. "Why, only last week there was a tramp that sneaked in and swiped the evening paper off the stoop, and she took off after him like a deer!"

Smiling at the compliment, and off the subject, my mother said, "And when do you have to go back to the City, Tommy?"

"Tomorrow," I said. "I'm going to look in at Governor Beal's mansion to see if anyone knows anything about Bobby Morton."

....

It was a grand mansion, no doubt of that, a fenced-in city block of it that could hold its head up on Nob Hill if its vast bulk with its towers and cupolas and dormers and balconies all in carpenter Gothic could be moved there. The former governor and his wife were visiting her relatives in France, but I was taken into the kitchen, which was the size of a ball field, for a cup of tea. The cook was Mrs. Anderson, a plump woman of fading prettiness who was pleased to have someone to chat with.

She remembered Robert Morton well, and had been hurt that he had departed one day without a farewell.

"Such a noice young man," she said, holding her teacup in both hands. "Such noice manners. He sang in the choir at Trinity Church, over on J Street, and he was a help to me and Mr. Gage and Mrs. Gaskell around the house."

She put her cup down and used both hands to illustrate Bobby Morton's departure. "Just, one day, gone! We told the sheriff about it in case there was foul play, but he didn't find out anything."

"Can you recall when this was?"

"It was when Governor Beal was opening the new racetrack, so it was a year ago April."

"What exactly did he do here?"

"Helped around the house, moving things, helping to fix things. He wasn't a handyman, but he was always cheerful and helpful. Mr. Gage didn't think as highly of him as Mrs. Gaskell and I did; he thought him rather a nancy-boy. But Mr. Gage is very gruff that way. I do hope Bobby is all right!"

"Is there a menagerie here?" I asked. "His grandmother mentioned something about a march of bears. Any bears?"

"No bears," she said, shaking her head, puzzled. "Birds, of course. Years ago there was a noice deer park, with a couple of deer, but that was years ago."

She apologized for not being able to show me the rest of the magnificent mansion, but Mr. Gage was very strict.

Mrs. Anderson did walk with me in the gardens, which were protected from N Street by a high wrought-iron fence of spear points. Trees bore little cards that gave their names in Latin. Planting beds had borders of bricks stacked in at a slant around them. There was no bear pen that I could see. Robert Morton remained a mystery.

I took the early afternoon train back to the City.

CHAPTER THIRTEEN

FORGETFULNESS, n. A gift of God bestowed upon debtors in compensation for their destitution of conscience.
—The Devil's Dictionary

THURSDAY, FEBRUARY 25, 1892

Bierce and Sam Chamberlain and I had been summoned to Willie Hearst's office. No doubt Willie wanted the Devine-Jaspers murder investigations to move more swiftly than they were moving, but he was careful not to say so for fear that Bierce would resign—as he did regularly, only to be coaxed back into the *Examiner* fold.

"Is there progress to report, Mr. Bierce?" was the way he got around to the subject. He sat behind his desk, with his pale, long face bisected by his narrow nose, and his perfectly combed hair bisected by its part, gazing nervously at Bierce. Sam Chamberlain sat with his arms folded and legs crossed as though he had tied himself into a loose knot, in his fine pin-striped suit and high collar, carnation in his buttonhole, monocle hanging from its cord.

"There is some speculation here, and some fact," Bierce said. "And no clear connection of the murder of Henry Devine to that of William Jaspers." He related what we had uncovered of Jaspers's history.

"He divorced his errant wife after the trial, and her life pursued a downward course until her death by consumption. She had married a worthless fellow named Morton, and her son, by Jaspers or Larrikin, took that name.

"My speculation is that Robert Morton was filled with the mother's bitter complaints against the life that had treated her so badly—and especially against William Jaspers, who had begun her downfall—that the son was raised in a climate of remembered and induced fury against the first husband who had initially ruined his mother. That when he read in last Thursday's *Examiner* that Jaspers was the Edwards of the murder twenty years ago, he determined to avenge the sins against his mother."

"One might further speculate that the young man resides in the *Examiner*'s circulation area," Sam said.

"I would presume he is in the City," Bierce said.

"What a story his pursuit will make!" Willie Hearst said, hands clasped together before his cravat.

"Will *not* make at this time," Bierce said, shaking his head. "As I have said, much of this is speculation. The last he was heard of, Robert Morton was employed at the Beal family mansion in Sacramento, in a peculiar role that sounds as though he cared for a menagerie of bears. This is being investigated, and may lead us to his current whereabouts."

"This is very intriguing, Mr. Bierce," Willie said.

"There is another line of reasoning that connects the two murders very well indeed," Bierce said. "Devine seduced any number of San Francisco women, many of them with wealthy husbands. William Jaspers then blackmailed the husbands for amounts measured to their degree of affluence. Tom and I have interviewed two. I spoke with a third, Isaac Thomas. He is a druggist with an establishment on Geary Street. The two others, who are more affluent than he, were tolerant of their wives' indiscretions. Not so Thomas, who railed at his wife in my presence until she burst into tears and fled the room. He pursued her, shouting after her. It was not a pleasant afternoon. He had been blackmailed for three hundred dollars, the other two for larger amounts."

"Will Jaspers," Sam said. "So a second wife also gave him horns. How was he provided with the essential information on her fellow seducees?"

"That's what I hope to find out shortly," Bierce said. "I do prefer the first line of investigation, as it does not involve such a large personnel."

"If further manpower is required to pursue the matter, I will make a squad of people available to you," Willie said.

Bierce just shook his head. "I believe this affair will reach its climax at the Suffrage Parade on Sunday."

"What climax would that be, Ambrose?" Sam said.

"It may be murderous in intent."

"And who would the victim be, Mr. Bierce?" Willie said.

Bierce did not turn his eyes toward me, and did not reply, but I knew he thought the victim might be one of the Trey of Pearls. After a pause he said, "I cannot speculate on that matter. But I believe I know the form the harrassment of the Suffragists will take."

"What would that be, Ambrose?"

"The phrase they are employing—the Monstrous Regiment of Women—is from the title of a diatribe by the sixteenth-century churchman John Knox. The entire title is 'The First Blast of the Trumpet Against the Monstrous Regiment of Women.' "

"Trumpets!" Sam said. *"Horns!"*

"Just so," Bierce said, and he said to me, "Tom, if you will relate the curious coincidences involving Mr. Frank Patchett."

I did so, Willie's and Sam's eyes fixed on me as I described my encounters with Jaspers's cashier.

"Why in the world would he be in Colfax?" Sam wanted to know.

"Again, I can only offer speculation," Bierce said. "There was some close connection between Patchett and William Jaspers. Patchett seems to have been the bill collector for blackmail in at least one instance. I think there was a relation, as though Patchett was trying to become William Jaspers. I suspect that Patchett is a relative of Jaspers's—possibly a son by some early misconduct. Or, in a way, he thinks of himself as Jaspers's son. So he was in Colfax by a coincidence that is really not that coincidental, on the same mission as Tom—looking for the son of Jaspers's first wife, who may have murdered his father."

Willie blew his breath out in a sigh. "I see you have many things to prove, Mr. Bierce."

"We do."

"How will you find out about that relation between Jaspers and this fellow?"

"I believe I will know that in a day or so."

Mammy Pleasant.

"We can only wish you well, Mr. Bierce, Mr. Redmond," Willie Hearst said.

"And Godspeed," Sam said.

"It may be," Bierce said, "that Tom and I will need assistance during the parade. Tom has firemen friends who can be called on. Others may be needed against ruffians, either E Clampus Vitas or adherents of a crazed preacher of a church on Washington Street."

"That can be arranged," Willie Hearst said. "Sam, will you put your thought to this personnel matter?"

"I will do that, Mr. Hearst," Sam said. "Horns!" he said. He sounded pleased.

....

Amanda and I sat across from each other at dinner at Malvolio's, surrounded by crisp napery and gleaming glassware. My Free Love cousin wore a dark suit with elaborate shoulder decorations and a generous bust I knew she could not actually fill. She was very quiet.

I assumed that my offer, or plea, or demand, or whatever it was, of marriage, did not need to be reiterated, and so instead opened the subject of my religion.

Amanda said firmly, "The Catholic Church maintains that a wife's first duty is to her husband's demands upon her!"

Taken aback, I said, "I didn't know that."

"Women know it."

"Amanda, you must believe I would not—"

"Ah, Cuz, I am sure you think you mean that!" She attempted her transcendent smile, but it was thin at the edges. Something was wrong. Maybe it was just the threat she and the other Pearls lived under, and next week's parade.

"I do mean that!"

"Cuz, I consider marriage a violation of self-sovereignty! You must believe it!"

"The normal relation between men and women who love each other—"

She would not let me finish. "You say it is normal! Is chattel slavery normal?"

"Amanda, it is not chattel slavery. It is a marriage of two equal souls who love each—"

"But you must see we cannot be equal by civil law or the laws of your Catholic Church!"

"But I love you!"

"Well, I love you, too, but it doesn't matter!"

It seemed voices must have been raised because adjacent diners were staring at us, and Signor Malvolio wandered near with a napkin stretched between his two hands as though it were his role to stifle us if we didn't quiet down.

Amanda plucked a stem of celery from the cut-glass bowl and crunched it between her small teeth. She consumed her celery noisily, in a manner of which I approved.

"Is that a Denver crunch?" I asked, to lighten our mood.

"It is an Amanda Wilson crunch," she replied. "I am crunching the bones of the priests and ministers who continue to seek to enslave women!"

"Please have an olive."

She did so, holding up a black olive. "The bones of cousins bent on seduction without conversion!"

"I am a convert!"

"Not to the abolition of conventional marriage!"

"That is true," I said. "I believe in marriage and in the children of marriage, for in the end that is what we are *for.* It is nature's way to forward the race of men."

"Ha!"

"And women!"

"It is religion's and the state's way. And men's. Not women's!"

Nearby diners were giving us irritated glances again.

"I have been converted to suffragism," I said.

A steaming bowl of pasta was placed before us, wine-glasses replenished. I gazed at my beautiful, angry cousin through the steam from the pasta platter. I saw that her eyes were blurred with tears, not with steam.

"What is it, Amanda?"

Her fingers plucked at a pocket in her bodice. She produced a folded bit of newsprint and handed it to me. I unfolded and read:

At the Russell Hall yesterday evening a Suffragist young woman rendered her opinions on the subjects of marriage and Free Love. From pretty young lips came ideas that were disgusting and obscene, arguments that would disgrace the tenants of a brothel. What she preached to the assembled women strikes at the peace, the security, and the very existence of society. She called for the abolition of all laws, civil and religious, that restrain relations between the genders.

It is inconceivable that the vile theories she advocated could find lodgment in any mind reasonably sane. They might, however, pervert the mind of youth by turning it into channels best avoided.

Are there no laws to govern the pronouncements of these vipers, who defy the decencies of American life? If there are not, I say we must recall the Vigilance Committee to clean out this Monstrous Regiment of Women.

This writer proposes just such a Committee with a declaration of principles drawn by Jesus-men with the intention of curing this abscess on the body of society. And if heroic means must be called upon to annihilate these Free Love anarchists and their allies the Suffragists, I say then what must be must be!

"Whew!" I said, handing it back to her, to be tucked back into her pocket. "Where is it from?"

"*The Evening Transcript*."

"It is the Reverend Stottlemyer," I said. "I know of him. Do you want me to beat the stuffing out of him?"

She shook her head. "It is the kind of thing your friend Mr. Bierce writes."

"Bierce writes with satire, and he does not advocate vigilante action!"

She pushed at the pasta, laid down her fork, and fixed me with her teary eyes.

"Amanda, you must know that your ideas raise a lot of hackles."

"He sounds like he wants to kill me!"

"He's just a blowhard."

"But are they planning to really try to hurt us at the parade?"

"They'd better not," I said, and thought myself a blowhard also. *Marry me and I will take you away from all this!* It was not the time for such an enunciation.

On the way home in the hack she allowed herself to be kissed, but would not come in. So I took her to the Cyrus Hotel and saw her inside, and then walked back to Sacramento Street.

As I stood in front of my door, at the top of the steps, key in hand, there was a whack of sound and splinters sprayed viciously off the door frame just above my head.

I ducked on shaky legs, turning to see a thin figure in an overcoat with his arm raised and the glint of the streetlamp off his revolver. I dropped into a huddle beside the balustrade of the steps, and he started down Sacramento Street at a gallop. I raised myself, vaulted down the steps, and lit out after him. He sprinted around the corner, headed toward Chinatown. When I got to the corner the block before me was empty, with a crowd of figures on the next block and some shrill Chinese music. A series of dark, recessed doorways confronted me, in any one of which my assailant might be concealed.

Still shaky-legged, I headed back the way I had come.

Someone had tried to kill me. I first thought it must be Frank Patchett, but it seemed that I had not offended him enough to warrant this.

CHAPTER FOURTEEN

ASPERSE, v. Maliciously to ascribe to another vicious actions which one has not had the temptation and opportunity to commit.
— The Devil's Dictionary

FRIDAY, FEBRUARY 26, 1892

Gertrude Atherton was with Bierce in his office, stooped behind him, looking over his shoulder—more instruction in prose style, I assumed. I was beckoned to remain. I didn't mind gleaning some hints on a fine style. Bierce had a thick half-leatherbound volume laid open on the desk before him, marked with protruding tabs of paper. His desk skull gaped outward.

"Battles are often won or lost on the quality of the commands generals issue to their subordinates," Bierce said to Mrs. Atherton, turning pages. "Whatever you may think of U. S. Grant as president of the Republic, he cannot be faulted on the quality of his commands as general. Here's one to General Blair: 'Move in early dawn toward Black River Bridge. I think you will encounter no enemy by the way. If you do, however, engage them at once.' "

He opened the book to another tab. "This to General McClernand: 'The entire force of the enemy has crossed the

Big Black. Disencumber yourself of your train, select an eligible position, and feel the enemy.'

"One more, To General McPherson: 'Pass all trains and move forward to join McClernand with all possible dispatch.'

"See how much action there is in these verbs?" he said to Mrs. Atherton. " 'Move, encounter, engage, disencumber, select, pass, feel, move again.' Simple, strong verbs, without adverbs. Few adjectives and fewer adverbs, my dear Mrs. Atherton. There is much to be learned here!"

"My dear Ambrose, I am not writing of battles or formations!"

Mrs. Atherton straightened to smile at me, and posed against the window behind her. I noticed that it was always her right profile that was presented. She wore a white blouse with considerable lace decoration, and a black skirt.

Bierce said, "I believe you told me once you wrote of the battles of the human spirit—in novels, of which you know I disapprove, novelists being particularly long-winded."

"I wonder if you mean me in particular, Ambrose."

"You are not particular, Gertrude."

Mrs. Atherton clucked. "Yes, Ambrose, and you have informed me that the shortest sentence possible is 'I am,' the longest is 'I do.'

"He says I must improve my prose style, Tom," she said to me. "He requires 'precision of thought, condensation, and individuality of expression.' He has written me a note to that effect! And he has given me the most weighty books to read: Walter Landor's *Imaginary Conversations*. A professor's *English Composition*, Longinius on 'The Sublime!' "

Bierce called her back to her lessons. I saw he had her manuscript on his desktop beneath the volume of Grant's *Personal Memoirs*.

"I must warn you on Latinate words also, Gertrude," he said. "Latinate words are polysyllabic, longer than their Anglo-Saxon equivalents, with a stress on the last syllable, such as 'transmit,' and 'desist.' The monosyllabic Anglo-Saxon equivalents 'send' and 'stop' are more forceful, and more effective. Latinate words are often used as euphemism for blunter Anglo-Saxonisms."

He leaned back in his chair, swiveling slightly so as to look up at Mrs. Atherton, and intoned: "I returned and saw under the sun, that the race is not to the swift, nor yet riches to men of understanding, nor yet favor to men of skill—"

"Yes, Ambrose, there is no doubt you are a man of skill," Mrs. Atherton said, skittishly. She smiled again at me, and said "I am enduring my daily lesson, Tom!"

"Well, I expect he is probably mostly right," I said.

"I am aware of that, of course," she said. She circled the desk and proceeded briskly out, calling back, "Thank you so much, Ambrose!"

Bierce gazed at me smugly over his templed fingertips. I gathered that his campaign for Mrs. Atherton's favors by way of her manuscript was proceeding well.

"Somebody tried to kill me last night," I said.

His eyes widened under his fierce eyebrows.

I explained. "About a foot lower and a little to the right would have done it."

"For what possible reason?" he said.

"I thought of Frank Patchett, but there doesn't seem reason enough."

"Can it be that someone thinks we are close to solving this complicated matter?"

"If Patchett thought I had uncovered something incriminating in Colfax—"

Bierce propped his fingertips together again. "Even if you did not, if he thought you had . . . What could it be?"

I searched through my recollections of my time in Colfax.

Bierce said, "I have ascertained that Dora McCall Morton is indeed deceased. She died on April 2, 1885. She was then just thirty-one years of age. The possibility had occurred to me that the wronged wife had come upon your piece in the *Examiner*, and her fury at her treatment had revived."

"Robert Morton remains a mystery. Does he really exist?"

"Patchett was surely on the same mission as you were."

"You think he tried to kill me?"

"I can think of no one else. There may be deeper levels to this investigation, however."

"I hope his aim does not improve," I said. "What about Devine?"

"Devine was killed because he had taken the wrong person to that couch in his office."

Frowning at me, he said, "Marching the bears. Or *osos,* where the verb in Spanish would be much the same as in English. What can that mean?"

I had no idea.

....

I was summoned back to his office by one of the corps of messenger boys who hung around the *Examiner* offices, this one in knee breeches and a torn sweater. Mammy Pleasant was there, basket in her lap, keen face thrust out of her bonnet like a weapon. She greeted me with a nod as I seated myself.

"Mrs. Pleasant has made some discoveries," Bierce said.

"Frank Patchett is probably the natural son of Edward Sayles, who became William Jaspers," Mammy said. She hesitated in order to give her announcement extra weight.

"His mother was an octoroon name of Milly Patchett. In St. Louis. She was a great beauty. Sayles was either married to her or not."

There was a loaded pause while Mammy tested whether either of us—probably me because she trusted Bierce—was thrown off balance at the thought of Negro blood. Certainly the very idea seemed to drive some otherwise sensible people right off their tracks.

The probability was that Frank Patchett and Robert Morton were half-brothers. The reason Patchett had been in Colfax was indeed the same as mine.

"It may be he used blackmail to get the job at the Cumberland Bank," Mammy continued. "Maybe not. He was devoted to his father. Spaniel dog devoted, they say. Son wanted to be just like the father, father flattered by it." She shrugged her thin shoulders in her shawl.

"Mother is dead?" Bierce asked.

"Dead."

"So he's Jaspers's heir," I said.

Both of them nodded.

"Who would be concerned about another heir," I said. "Which might identify my shooter."

"You were the only one he missed," Bierce said, adding, "Captain Chandler will know if Jaspers died intestate."

....

Bierce inflated his cheeks, blew out a sigh, shook his head, and said, "Marching with bears."

I shook my head.

"I wonder if a breakfast could be arranged," he said. "You and I and the Trey. At the Palace."

"I don't know if we can get them away from Mrs. Quinan."

"It is important," Bierce said.

"Breakfast with Pearls," I said.

"Yes."

....

A packet of papers had arrived from my father: a *Sacramento Bee* column of disgusting pap describing the wonders of Governor Beal's estate in Sacramento, which I glanced over with impatience at the self-congratulatory aspect of Sacramentans, and put aside to show Bierce; and a note from the gent:

Tommy, your six-and-a-half-foot preacher was a clergyman at a B Street Church in Stockton named Cosmo Tate. He fled town on an embezzlement charge, which is still open on the Stockton police books.

Your mother inquires regarding progress on the marriage and grandchild front.

Your faithful informant & father, Cletus Redmond.

It was with pleasure that I took these documents down the hall to Bierce's office.

....

In the corridor outside the rooms where Mrs. Quinan and the Trey were ensconced, Patrolman Peterson, arms akimbo, barred the way to a burly gent wearing a derby hat and stabbing a finger at Peterson's blue, eight-button tunic.

"Patchett!" I said.

He swung toward me, jut-jawed, and went into a crouch as though expecting an assault. I felt this gave me a leg up on him.

"Told him he is not going in there to threaten those females!" Peterson said. He had a face like a rubber Irish toy beneath his helmet.

"Robert Morton!" I said, like a password.

Patchett straightened, although he still gripped his right wrist in his left hand as though to repel boarders. His deepset eyes regarded me with hostility.

"We were in Colfax on the same mission," I said. "Looking for your half-brother."

"What's that you say?"

Patrolman Peterson, who seemed to feel the situation was under control, retreated two steps. The gas light behind him hissed and flared.

"Did you take a shot at me last night?" I asked.

Patchett's eyebrows shot up.

I thought he had not.

"Robert Morton is your father's other son," I said.

"He is Oscar Larrikin's get!"

"And you think he killed your father. Jaspers."

"My *father*?" he said.

"The man whose wife was seduced by Larrikin, and who killed him for it, was named Edwards. Before that his name was Edward Sayles. Your father and Robert Morton's father. Two heirs."

He retreated a step. His face was a study, and I hoped Mammy had been correct. Patrolman Peterson regarded us over his folded arms.

Patchett didn't want to talk about paternity.

"Did you find out where he went to?" he said.

"Worked on Governor Beal's estate in Sacramento for a while, then he cut out. What are you doing here?"

"Trying to get these Suffragist women to cancel their parade."

"Why should they?"

"The Clampers are going to roust them! It'll be a hash!

There'll be humiliations done. I want to save them a big mess, you see."

"So you have taken over Jaspers's position."

He shook his head. "Another chap. Not me. I mean, they are determined on it. There's been meetings, and plans."

"Horns?" I said, but he did not respond to that.

"I'll tell you what Mrs. Quinan will say," I went on. "Why is it that the women have to give way so as not to have big, humiliating trouble? Is there talk of violence?"

Patchett sighed. I thought I had better revise my opinion of him.

"Listen, Redmond, there are some Clampers that really *hate* the women's movement. You've heard this thing they say, Monstrous Regiment of Women?"

I took a quick breath. "From the Reverend Stottlemyer?"

"I don't know where it came from. I just hear it from chaps I know. There is some dead-set on trouble, you see."

"And you'd like to prevent that?"

"I think it's a bad thing, but I see what you mean; Madame Quinine would say why do *they* have to give way?"

"Because it must've come up just like this many times before. Women, being women, are supposed to give way."

He nodded once, shook his head once, backed off another step.

I said, "I am welcome here, and I will tell them just what you have to say. Will that suffice you?"

"Well, yes, I guess so. Thanks, Redmond. Sorry about the other day." He turned and stalked away down the hall, a burly, broad-shouldered fellow whom I had almost forgotten was part Negro.

....

"I will say, you did calm that fellow down," Patrolman Peterson said.

"A kind word turneth away wrath," I said, surprised to hear myself saying it. "I didn't think he so much wanted to frighten them as that he was frightened for them."

"If you say so, Mister."

"I've come to call," I said.

"Reckon you are all right." He beckoned me past.

I was to issue an invitation to breakfast with Bierce and me at the Palace Hotel to Amanda, Gloria, and Emmiline.

I was sure that Mrs. Quinan would not be persuaded to cancel the Suffrage Parade by threats of humiliation and violence, but I passed along Patchett's warning anyhow, as Mme. Starr's queen of spades and pair of fours lurked in a corner of my mind like a rattlesnake.

CHAPTER FIFTEEN

INGRATE, n. One who receives a benefit from another, or is otherwise an object of charity.

— The Devil's Dictionary

SUNDAY, FEBRUARY 28, 1892

There was an item in Sunday's "Prattle" that gave me some personal satisfaction:

One of the noisiest of the Protestant Birds of Pray of this unsaintly city is the Reverend George Stottlemyer of the Washington Street All-Jesus Church. Among his many ecclesiastical honors was his ministry in the B Street Evangelical Church of Jesus in Stockton, from which fine city he made his way here, trailing charges of embezzlement and wrongful appropriation. Chief of Police Homer B. Johnson of that city, contacted by telephone, says that if San Francisco's Rev Stottlemeyer is a beanpole of a fellow who calls himself Jesus-man, his fat is fried.

There was also some sniping between Gertrude Atherton and Bierce.

From "Woman in Her Variety":

All short-story writers are jealous of novelists. They all try to write novels, and few of them succeed. Any clever, cultivated mind with a modicum of talent can manage a short story. But it takes a very special endowment and abundant imagination to sustain the creative faculty throughout a story of novel length.

From "Prattle":

With rare exceptions, women who write fiction are destitute of the sense of right and wrong. Never have I known a female novelist who did not lie and cheat with as little concern as a pig with a mouthful of larks.

I wondered if this exchange denoted a quarrel or a closer relation between the two Sunday columnists. They were both hard on women, Mrs. Atherton as much so as Bierce. Although she disapproved of adultery, as she had announced to Amanda, she was against marriage, especially if it lasted too long, with incompatability the great marital evil. Divorce was certainly more honorable than a loveless marriage, and if divorce was impossible, there was always murder. She had pursued the subject of spousal disposal in rather shocking detail one Sunday, recommending serving the incompatible husband wine loaded with ground glass, or stabbing him in the eardrum with a knitting needle.

....

Headed for the Palace Hotel for breakfast with three young women tripping along beside us pleased Bierce very much. While disparaging of their gender, Bierce did enjoy pretty females. The three wore their sparkling white Suffragist uniforms with black belts looped around narrow waists.

Bierce was well turned out also in fine black suiting, a roseate cravat, gleaming boots, and hard hat cocked at an angle on his curly, graying head. Amanda was not so touchful as usual, among her associates, but walked close beside me and laughed up into my face, with Bird Girl beside her and Emmiline beside Bierce, nodding in conversation with him.

Bierce's idea of breakfast had allowed Mrs. Quinan to be left behind, for she was a late sleeper on Sunday mornings.

At the Palace Hotel, breakfast was served from a sideboard in the grand dining room, awash with sunlight from the skylights. We were urged to partake of Bierce's favorite Palace specialty—oysters and eggs. Amanda and Bird Girl heaped their plates with this mess also, while Emmiline and I, in gestures of independence, chose the omelette and rashers of bacon. We were seated in close company at a four-person table, and coffee was brought in a steaming silver pot. Bierce looked around at his pretty companions with a pleased expression.

"The Trey of Pearls!" he exclaimed.

"Here at your beck, Mr. Bierce!" Bird Girl said, as her otherworldly eyes gazed in awe about the great room.

Emmiline picked at her eggs with her fork. "So much light!"

"Let there be light!" Amanda said.

"You are from Denver, I understand, Miss Wilson?"

"Yes, I am. I am the granddaughter of Tom Redmond's father's older sister."

"That is as complicated as Amanda is!" Emmiline said.

"And you, Miss Prout?"

"I am an easterner. From Pittsburgh, although there we think of Pittsburgh as western."

Gloria Robinson was from Austin, Nevada, where her

father was sheriff. "One of the first families of Austin!" she said in her sprightly way. "My grandfather ran for governor but received only twenty-four votes!"

Emmiline and Amanda giggled at this, with side glances at each other that caused me to think that Gloria was not always truthful in her assertions.

Bierce tucked in his napkin and engaged his oysters and eggs. I said to Emmiline, "Where did you meet Mrs. Quinan?"

"In Pittsburgh, where she spoke some years ago. My mother and father are abolitionists, so I was brought up to think in terms of *causes.* Mrs. Quinan provided a cause."

"Me as well," Amanda said. "Or should I have said 'I as well,' Mr. Bierce?"

"I will let Mr. Redmond settle that," Bierce said.

"Unfortunately, I as well as you are often confused by grammar," I said.

Amanda laughed merrily. Bird Girl regarded me with her strange eyes. "But you are also a newspaperman, Mr. Redmond."

"We prefer the term journalist."

"My uncle is a journalist in Pittsburgh," Emmiline said. "Although I believe in Pittsburgh the term 'newspaperman' is allowed."

"And you, Miss Wilson, where did you encounter Mrs. Quinan?"

"She is a friend of my mother's. My mother is also a Suffragist."

"But not a Free Lover of the varietist persuasion, I would imagine."

Amanda raised her head upright, chin out, color in her cheeks, pretty lips pursed. "That is correct, Mr. Bierce."

"Mandy always has to be first at everything," Bird Girl said.

"That's not true, Glory!"

Holding his coffee cup, Bierce said, "And you, Miss Robinson?"

"I heard her speak. She was with Mrs. Cullen and Miss Braverman. It was a grand feminist rally!"

"In Austin?"

"Oh, no, Austin is a tiny camp. In Denver. I had gone there with my mother and father for another business. I met Mandy there." I thought Bird Girl wore a touch of rouge on her lips. The other two did not.

"And have there been other ruckuses like the one the Clampers promise here?"

"Yes, there have been, Mr. Bierce," Emmy said. Her tight little mouth was drawn into a pout, her perfect forehead marred by a dipping frown line. "We have been fortunate to have gentlemen on hand who quelled them."

"Glory sings," Amanda said. "If they are very obstreperous she sings 'The Star-Spangled Banner,' to which they must repond respectfully."

The notion of rowdies brought up short by the national anthem pleased me, and the fact that the Trey had survived previous rousts relieved me.

"You may know there have been threats other than Mr. Jaspers's and Mr. Patchett's," Bierce said.

"That is why Patrolman Peterson guards your hallway," I said.

"There are always *threats*," Amanda said. A foot, which I presumed to be hers, prodded mine.

"Are they from men who object to your public utterances?"

"Mandy's utterance the most," Bird Girl said. "My bird calls could be male or female, after all, and Emmy is so ladylike."

"We are all supposed to be ladylike," Emmiline said, "Being Pearls."

"And very comely Pearls at that," Bierce said.

"I am the most threatened Pearl," Amanda said. "I don't know that it is utterance that causes men to threaten us. It may be just the fact of *us.*"

"Especially you, though, Mandy," Bird Girl said. She gave Amanda a mischievous look, but Amanda did not appear amused.

The case seemed to be that Bird Girl teased Amanda rather clumsily, which Amanda did not appreciate, and Emmiline ignored it. Amanda squinted prettily up at the light streaming through the ceiling panes. I loved her. I wanted to marry her, and have by her one child to satisfy my mother. After that it would be her choice. I thought if she continued to refuse me I would be so downcast I would begin teasing her clumsily, like Bird Girl.

"We are all loyal to Mrs. Quinan," Amanda said.

Bierce said, "It is thought, indeed, that your Free Love utterances are derived from her personal escutcheon."

"Who thinks that?" Amanda said with mock severity. "Tom Redmond? He doesn't know anything about feminist matters."

"Mandy is Mrs. Quinan's favorite," Bird Girl said.

"No, I am not, Glory!"

"Because she is also Free Love."

"You are her favorite because you need the most instruction in being ladylike."

"Emmiline is her favorite because she is already the most ladylike. You are just a rowdy Denver fancy speaker."

Amanda cocked a little fist and threatened Bird Girl with it until both were laughing. Emmiline Prout looked disapprovingly at the horseplay.

And a good time was had by all, until breakfast was done and Bierce and I escorted the three young ladies back to their hotel. I didn't know what we had learned other than that there was a considerable amount of friction, as well as affection, among the Trey, and, deep in thought, Bierce did not seem to wish to discuss the matter.

"I can only think of marching bears," he groaned.

....

As soon as we had returned to the *Examiner*, Mrs. Atherton swept into Bierce's office.

"Ambrose!" she cried. Her beautiful face was tragic. "Willie Hearst has acquired some letters of Ella Wheeler Wilcox!"

"Has he?" Bierce said, retreating behind his desk as though to protect himself from Mrs. Atherton. I knew Ella Wheeler Wilcox as a maudlin and sentimental poet and advice-giver, whose advice, presented in one of the New York papers, counseled women in exactly the opposite direction from that of Mrs. Atherton in "Woman in Her Variety."

"The idea is that one of her perfectly dreadful letters will be published, and I will respond to it. I will not stand for it, Ambrose. She is my enemy!"

"I didn't think she had enough spunk to be anyone's enemy."

Mrs. Atherton placed her hands on the desktop beside the skull and leaned toward Bierce. She was shaking with anger. "I will not stand for this, Ambrose! It is an insult!"

"Calm down a moment, please, Gertrude," Bierce said. He signaled me with his eyebrows, and I departed.

....

The two women had had a quarrel in New York, Bierce told me later.

Ella Wheeler Wilcox had published a bestselling book of

poetry, *Poems of Passion*, at the same time that Mrs. Atherton's novel *Hermia Suydam* was being labeled "prurient" and "scandalous" by New York critics.

Mrs. Wilcox's counsel to women was indeed exactly opposed to Mrs. Atherton's; ideal women were shy and innocent, devoted mothers, all tact and modesty in their relations with men. Mrs. Atherton had attacked her in print as having mousy hair, to which the poetess had responded that Mrs. Atherton's blond mane came out of a bottle. There had been headlines on the matter in the *Examiner* before Mrs. Atherton had arrived back in San Francisco:

DAGGERS AND HAIRPINS

**ELLA WHEELER WILCOX
AND GERTRUDE ATHERTON**

THE PRIESTESS OF PASSION SAYS
SOMEBODY BLEACHES HER HAIR

Bierce was vastly amused at this female quarrel, and at Mrs. Atherton's rage, which served to confirm his opinions of the gender. At the same time I knew that he was concerned that the present situation might result in Mrs. Atherton leaving the *Examiner*, for she had the option of declaring herself a novelist instead of a journalist.

I learned that he had also done some detective work connected with our breakfast.

"There is no record of a sheriff named Robinson in Austin, Nevada," he said. "Nor have I been able to track down a family of abolitionists by the name of Prout in Pittsburgh. Can it be that these Pearls have joined their leader out of thin air?"

"I can vouch only for the existence and the ancestry of my cousin," I said.

CHAPTER SIXTEEN

MAD, adj. Affected with a high degree of intellectual independence; not conforming to standards of thought, speech and action derived by the conformants from study of themselves; at odds with the majority; in short, unusual.

— *The Devil's Dictionary*

SUNDAY, FEBRUARY 28, 1892

Bierce and I were invited to a picnic on Angel Island aboard Willie Hearst's steam launch *Aquila*. Others aboard were Mrs. Quinan, Mrs. Atherton, Sam Chamberlain, and Willie's mother, Mrs. George Hearst, widow of the mining magnate and U.S. senator. We sat opposite each other on the fancily upholstered seats of the *Aquila,* a varnished mahogany canopy protecting us from the sun. Willie stood at the wheel, legs spread apart, in his blue double-breasted jacket and white trousers, captain's cap aslant his neatly combed hair. I had not had occasion to discuss with Bierce the purpose of this outing, but it might be to heal Willie's breech with Mrs. Atherton over the scheme to set her into conflict with Ella Wheeler Wilcox in the Sunday edition.

Mrs. Hearst was in earnest conversation with Mrs. Quinan, who wore her Suffragist white under a dustcatcher greatcoat, and a naval-looking hat. Mrs. Hearst was surely no more than five feet tall but appeared taller due to a straight back and a proud, upright head in a broad-brimmed hat outlined against the sun on the Bay. She had a chin and jaw as determined as those of the Suffragist chieftain. They were in fact a formidable female pair.

Although the *Examiner,* which Senator Hearst had presented to his son, was now in the black, Willie lived on a very expensive scale, with a mansion in Sausalito called Sea Point, where he kept his mistress. Willie's employees were certain that Mrs. Hearst would ultimately win the war to rid Willie of pretty Tessie Powers, simply because she controlled the Hearst bank accounts.

Mrs. Atherton sulked in her seat next to Sam Chamberlain, her fine profile raised, a scarf over her perhaps-bottle-bleached hair. Bierce and I sat on either side of Willie at the wheel.

"We have made no progress," Bierce told him. "I do know what Captain Chandler believes, which is the simplest explanation, as is common with police cogitation. He believes that the Reverend Devine was murdered by William Jaspers because Devine had seduced his wife. And he believes that the ensuing issue of the *Examiner,* which revealed Jaspers's previous murder of a wife's lover, resulted in the murder of Jaspers by the son of that first wife—either his or the lover's offspring. And that murderer is either among us, or has departed for Tierra del Fuego. And there it stands."

"And do you agree with that assessment, Mr. Bierce?"

"Let me say that we do not have a better solution."

"Should we then call off this investigation?"

"We are waiting for something further to happen," Bierce said.

Willie adjusted the wheel an eighth of a turn. No doubt he was thinking of a Gee Whiz front page.

"We are awaiting the Suffragist Parade," Bierce said.

"My mother will be marching," Willie said, nodding toward Mrs. Hearst. "But she does not wish any newspaper notice of her participation."

Sam Chamberlain had Mrs. Atherton smiling at his jokes. Willie's Chinese boy, Wong, had taken a bottle from one of the picnic hampers and was pouring champagne. The *Aquila* pitched in a slight chop. Another steam launch, a mile away, was proceeding on a parallel course. Beyond it were a steamer and a sailing ship with a high rack of masts and spars under tow. They were cut off by the cliffs of Alcatraz Island.

Holding her champagne glass, Mrs. Quinan came to sit beside me, while Mrs. Hearst joined Sam Chamberlain and Mrs. Atherton.

Mrs. Quinan's sagging face seemed cinched up by the black velvet band around her throat.

"Amanda is much troubled by your attentions, Mr. Redmond," she said, very schoolmarmish.

My own opinion, which I kept to myself, was that Amanda was pleased by my attentions.

"You must understand that she is not free to marry."

"I wonder why she is not," I said.

"Because she has vowed her allegiance to our cause, Mr. Redmond."

"Why can't she have allegiance to your cause and be married also?"

She regarded me as though I were an idiot. "Mr. Redmond, her role is dependent upon being a questioner of marriage, not a participant in it."

"Then that role is against her nature."

She fumbled for her pince-nez spectacles and donned them so as to examine me more closely. Her eyes enlarged at me like goldfish approaching in a bowl.

"We will change human nature if we must."

"I doubt that, Mrs. Quinan."

"You are an enemy, then."

"You will find I am not an enemy when you count your supporters against the Clampers at the parade next week."

"Then I can only wish for dear Amanda not to be troubled by your importunities."

"I think she is not troubled, but gratified."

"Nonsense!" She gave me a severe look, rose, and left me.

Willie nosed the *Aquila* to a rickety little dock on the Angel Island shore. The men handed the ladies onto the dock while Wong wrestled with the picnic baskets. Bierce seated himself beside Mrs. Atherton on a grassy bank and I joined them. I perceived that he was in competition with Sam Chamberlain for her favors, if there were any to be had.

"Let me caution you about the habitual use of the habitual case," he was advising her. "When 'would' is used, nothing is actually happening. It is a generalized happening, not a specific one. 'Would' is indefinite and unparticular."

"Thank you, Ambrose," she said. "I will certainly be less habitual in the future."

Willie ambled over in his blue blazer and captain's cap, to squat uncomfortably beside Mrs. Atherton. He was frowning, his long pale face with its bisecting nose like a kind of caricature of itself.

"Ah, Mrs. Atherton," he said. "I understand you are not pleased with the arrangement I have made regarding Mrs. Wilcox's letters."

"That is correct, Mr. Hearst," she said. She had crossed her arms tightly over her bosom, and gazed back at him tight-lipped.

"I am very sorry to hear that."

"She represents everything about the feminine gender that I oppose, Mr. Hearst."

"But that is exactly what I had in mind, Mrs. Atherton. With her letters, and your column to be written in response to them—her opinions are rather sitting ducks, don't you see?"

"Mrs. Wilcox is a great practitioner of the habitual case," Bierce said.

Mrs. Atherton smiled despite herself. Willie continued his persuasions. Fried chicken and potato salad were served, champagne corks popped. Sam Chamberlain, tall and thin in his fancy cream-colored suiting, with a carnation in his buttonhole, tended to Mrs. Hearst and Mrs. Quinan and cast glances toward those of us seated on the bank.

Willie continued to discourse on the pleasures Mrs. Atherton would have attacking Ella Wheeler Wilcox's sentimental effusions, and Mrs. Atherton, seeming to relent, regaled Sam Chamberlain, Bierce, and Willie with tales of her late husband.

"George was proudest of events in which he had taken part in his youth," she said. "How he loved to boast of these exploits, and the musical disasters he had caused. There were Sunday brass-band concerts near where he lived, and he and his rascally friends would attend these and suck on lemons and pickles before the horn players because, of course, the sight of someone sucking on a pickle causes such a collection of saliva to form sympathetically in the hornblower's mouth that he simply cannot blow! George was very proud of these rebellions against a strict upbringing. In his cups, he would never fail to tell the grand story—with sound effects! Poor dear, he really didn't have much else to boast about."

"Unlike his beautiful and talented spouse," Bierce said, without apparent irony.

....

After lunch we clustered on the bank and sang the songs Mrs. Hearst, acting as musical director, chose for us. Mrs. Quinan regretted that we did not have Gloria Robinson on hand to lead us in "The Battle Hymn of the Republic," but we sang it, badly, anyway. Bierce did not participate in the singing.

About two o'clock we packed up and reembarked on the *Aquila* and racketed back to the Clay Street wharf, still singing.

When we had disembarked, Bierce stood beside the hack I had hailed while the hackie unwound his whip from the handle. Bierce said unhappily, "I am afraid Mrs. Atherton is not long for the *Examiner.*"

"I thought Willie was persuasive."

"I believe she is talking herself into novelist mode, and will presently decide to disdain journalism."

"Too bad," I said.

"I am not sure that is a loss to journalism," Bitter Bierce said.

"Ah!"

"One does wonder if those were the only horns that poor George Atherton was exposed to."

....

I had not been at home ten minutes when there was a tattoo of knocks and Amanda burst in. I was seated before my typewriter, switching around to face her, and before I could rise she had plumped herself down on my lap with her face pressed into my neck. I embraced her.

"Tom!" she whispered. "I know who killed Henry Devine!"

"Who?"

"I can't tell you!"

"Then tell me what is the use of your prancing in here announcing you know who killed Devine but can't say who?"

"He did it because of me!"

"Because you made free with Devine?"

"Yes!"

"Is he someone you have been free with also?"

"No more than you and me!"

I squeezed her to show that none of this mattered to me, when of course it did. Whoever had killed Henry Devine had also tried to kill me! And what of her?

"I've made such a mess of everything, Tom. I'm such a *fraud*."

"I know that."

"Not that way!" She detached herself so I could see her tear-stained face, which I loved, scowling at my presumption.

I said, "If he is someone you have had a relation with in the past surely we can find out who he is."

"You can't! Unless I—" She stopped.

"Does he know you know?"

"No! But I will tell him. I will persuade him that he must turn himself in to Mr. Bierce."

"Then you will be in danger!"

She thrust her face into my neck again. "What must I do, Tom?"

"I can't say what you must do unless I know who he is, and where you stand with him."

She was shaking her head as I spoke.

"I love you," I said.

"I love you too!"

"Marry me!"

"No!"

I kissed her damp face.

She whispered, "Don't you *want* me, Tom?"

"After we are married."

Fatal words.

She would not tell me who he was or what she had discovered; she only wept and blamed herself.

I took her home to the Cyrus Hotel and saw her inside, and returned to my rooms.

CHAPTER SEVENTEEN

ABASEMENT, n. A decent and customary mental attitude in the presence of wealth or power.

— The Devil's Dictionary

MONDAY, MARCH 1, 1892

There was an itch of conscience that I was betraying Amanda's confidences with Bierce, but lives were at stake.

He said, "Do you think she can be persuaded to disclose this fellow's identity?"

I didn't think so. "She said she would persuade him to turn himself in to you."

"No hint?"

"None."

"No doubt Captain Chandler can make contact with his equivalent in Denver to discover her lovers."

"She seemed sure that we couldn't find out who he was. So he is someone we would never suspect."

Bierce thought about that.

"Meanwhile he is not in Denver, he is in San Francisco with his overcoat and cloth cap and revolver."

"And knows the movements and habits of your beloved."

"Yes!"

"He and the two murderers must be the same person."

"Robert Morton?"

"Is Amanda Wilson's jealous lover." Bierce leaned forward to rearrange the skull on his desk, so that it gazed past me vacantly.

I said, "I can't think straight when this is so close to the woman I have asked to marry me."

"Marching *osos,*" he said. "Can marching bears be equated with marching females?"

....

Mme. Starr's wagonette was still in the field beside the brick building, in the stink from the next-door slaughterhouse. In the field a boy and a girl were taking turns kicking an empty kerosene can, the girl emitting high-pitched shrieks of excitement.

Mme. Starr invited me in to the interior gloom. On her table were a candle in a whisky bottle and a plate with a half-eaten cheese sandwich on it. She disposed of this beneath the table, rearranged her hair within her head covering, and presented her greasily gleaming face in the candlelight.

"What can I do for you, mister?"

I explained that a former lover of my fiancée was very jealous, and that my fiancée and I had both been threatened. My fiancée was a member of the Suffragist Trey of Pearls. I wanted to know the identity of our enemy.

"Mr. Randolph?" Mme. Starr called softly. After a moment the candle flickered. I was prepared for this but couldn't make out how it was managed.

From outside I could hear the metallic whacks of the kicked can, and the girl's muted shrieks.

Mme. Starr explained the situation to her spirit guide. She produced her deck of cards, shuffled and reshuffled, and slung them out in a broad curve, one card detaching itself from the rest. I was breathing hard as she reached out a beringed hand to turn it over. The jack of hearts.

"What does that mean?" I demanded.

"A young man," she said. "Hearts is significant. A young person in love, or loved, somebody's son. Son of a queen, perhaps? Your enemy.

"Mr. Randolph?" she said again.

As though having received some directive inaudible to me, she gathered up the cards, shuffled and reshuffled, and flung them out again. Again one slid free of the rest. This proved to be the jack of clubs.

"Oh, clubs," she said, frowning as though there had been a misdeal. She called for Mr. Randolph again, but this time there was no response. We sat regarding the jack of clubs.

After a time Mme. Starr brightened. "It is there, young man," she said. "You will understand. If you believe, it will come to you."

I gave her three dollars for her trouble, and left her, trying to believe.

....

I knew who this young man was, sidling into my office with a cloth cap on his head and a close-cropped blond beard. He was Jake Burgess, the man friday of Marshall McGee, the Ambrose Bierce of the *Chronicle,* and so a kind of alter ego to me. For the *Chronicle* and the *Examiner* were in a ferocious circulation war, and successful innovations that young Willie Hearst brought to the newspaper business—such as reporters acting as detectives and murders as front-page Gee Whiz material—Mike DeYoung's *Chronicle* was bound to copy. And vice versa.

Of course Jake Burgess and Marshall McGee would be concerned with the Devine and Jaspers murders if Bierce and I were.

Jake flipped a hand to ask for a chair, and I flipped a hand to welcome him to it, though welcome was not what it was in my mind to express.

"So, Jake," I said.

"Jaspers. We have it there was a son, either his or Larrikin's, that's probably the perp we're all looking for."

"Where'd you get that idea?"

He showed me his crooked teeth in his narrow blond-bearded face. "Privileged information."

"Let me guess. Frank Patchett."

His eyes widened at me. "Jaspers's assistant and votary and move-in fellow and sub-devil? Devoted to his boss, and God's own scourge of loan delinquents."

It occurred to me that my own research might have been delinquent.

"Tell me, Tom. Any idea where Robert Morton might be?"

"San Francisco, or Tierra del Fuego, Bierce thinks."

He showed me his teeth again. "That's what Captain Chandler thinks. McGee doesn't think Bierce thinks what Captain Chandler thinks."

"What's McGee's theory?"

"We go along with Bobby Morton killing his father after he saw the spread in the *Examiner.* Don't see any doubts there, even though there is a host of loan delinquents out there would've liked to collect Jaspers's kidneys and feed them to the cat."

I had a picture of McGee and Jake as a kind of mirror image, or maybe shadow play, of Bierce and me, going through the same motions and coming to different and—surely!—erroneous conclusions.

"So where'll we find Bobby Morton, Tom?"

"Maybe he'll show up at the parade."

He leaned conspiratorially toward me, smelling of barbershop talcum and cologne. "Separate murders and murderers," he whispered.

"That's what McGee thinks?"

"That's what he thinks. Now. Miss Amanda Wilson, one of the Trey of Pearls. Suffragist beauty. Free Love speaker. Your cousin, they tell me."

"She is my cousin."

He goggled at me in what I supposed he thought was a comical fashion.

"Ha ha!" he said.

"What does that mean, Jake?"

"Means it is well known she and you is having a little doobooleedo."

"What does that peculiar word mean?"

"Ha ha!"

"You mean you think there is something besides cousinness between Miss Wilson and me? In fact, nothing beside cousinness exists."

"Ha ha!" he said, infuriatingly. He leered. Then he sobered. "Well, that is not the point I am here for, Tom. Her and Henry Devine. Doobooleedo."

If one was a known Free Lover, how did one dispute imputations of Free Love? I hoped I had composed my face properly.

"Not something we are working on," I said.

"*We* are."

"Go it," I said.

"Miss Wilson declines to speak to me."

"Her prerogative, surely."

"I hoped you would speak to her about speaking to me."

"I decline," I said.

"Makes it sound worse, you see. Evidence of guilt. Devine and you."

It seemed that Amanda's late nights in my rooms were known not only to the murderer.

"Jake," I said. "There is no reason for you to believe me, I suppose. But I will swear to you that on my part there has been no doobooleedo."

He frowned at me. "But why won't you intercede with Miss Wilson for me?"

"Because that is her business."

"You understand that what McGee writes about this in the *Chron* will be the worse for her if she do not cooperate."

"That may be," I said. "But you understand the weekend after this Wednesday's parade, she will be on the train for New York City and then a steamer to London on Suffragist business, and gone from San Francisco."

I had hardly confronted that fact myself.

Jake sucked on his teeth, gazing at me. "You understand if the *Examiner* is on one side of this Suffragist Parade, the *Chronicle* is bound to be on the other."

McGee in his column had referred to Mrs. Quinan's associates as "The Tray of Tarts."

"With the Clampers," I said.

"Monstrous Regiment of Women, etcetera!"

"Yes."

"I'm a Clamper, Tom. We're all Clampers at heart. Why aren't you?"

"Matter of discrimination, I guess."

"Tolerable *Examiner* discrimnation, oh, my, yes!"

I considered the *Chronicle*'s well-known proclivity for jumping over facts to reach desired conclusions, a procedure copied from the *Examiner*, they no doubt would claim.

"Frank Patchett's moved in at Jaspers's house, you know," Jake said.

"Is that so?"

"That's so. Exchange of info, Tom?"

I raised empty hands.

"Thanks for nothing," he said. He peeled himself out of my chair and was gone.

I sat there sorting through my emotions.

CHAPTER EIGHTEEN

RETALIATION, n. The natural rock upon which is reared the Temple of Law.

—The Devil's Dictionary

MONDAY, MARCH 1, 1892

Half a block up Taylor from Pine, the Jaspers mansion towered more vertical than horizontal on the steep slope with a veranda across the front, steep hipped roofs, and a tall chimney.

Bierce and I trudged up the paving stones. A maid in a starched apron answered the door. I asked for Mr Patchett, and we were shown upstairs to Jaspers's office. Patchett was seated at Jaspers's desk in his shirt sleeves, and rose scowling to greet us. He was Jaspers-bearded, with his hair neatly brushed from a part like a chalk line, and wearing a striped necktie and vest.

Hands clasped behind his back, Bierce prowled the room, gazing up at the high moldings with their solid rank of keepsakes and mementos.

"Looks like you are pretty well situated here," I said to Patchett, since Bierce had decided to be a silent partner. "Down at the bank also?"

"Little trouble with that old badger Stevens down there,"

he said, stretching with his arms out. He jacked up his scowl. "What do you want here, Redmond?"

"How's Mrs. Jaspers?"

"Grieving, of course. Mr. Jaspers was killed because of that piece of yours in the *Examiner*, you know that." He turned his scowl on Bierce, who was now gazing out a window, down Taylor Street.

"I thought he was killed because of paternities," I said. "Wasn't that why we were in Colfax? You even look like him, Patchett."

He seated himself again. "Will Jaspers was a man I looked up to more'n any other, that's all," he said. "Decided at some point I was going to be a man exactly like he was. Come up from humble beginnings to bank vice president. Married a fine woman. Lives in a fine house on Nob Hill."

It all must have looked very good to the son of Milly Patchett in St. Louis.

Bierce was still contemplating the view. "Sit down if you want," Patchett said with a wave.

"Where are you from originally, Patchett?" I asked.

"Don't ask that out West here, do we?" He grinned as though he'd held me up at second base. "St. Louis. Angel for a mother, father that lit out early. Three other kits. Jaspers was a kind of family friend there."

"I understand your father was known as Sayles then."

He stared at me as though he did not intend to answer, and then he jerked up out of his chair again. "Come in, Martha!"

Mrs. Jaspers swept in, wearing a black gown with a white collar, her white hands laid like decorations against her bosom. Beneath a pile of dark hair was a triangular white face with green eyes, a pink slit of a mouth. She was very pretty. I hurried to my feet also.

"You have visitors, Frank!"

Mrs. Jaspers, at least, had commanded Bierce's attention. He moved away from the window.

I said, "I'm Tom Redmond, Mrs. Jaspers. And you remember Mr. Bierce. We were here with Captain Chandler."

Patchett was regarding his stepmother with bright eyes, rather like Cortez viewing the Aztec capital from a nearby mountain.

Bierce still did not seem inclined to speak up, so I said, "I see your affairs are in good hands with Mr. Patchett here, Mrs. Jaspers."

"Mr. Patchett has been wonderful. So helpful. Such a comfort." Now she detached the white spiders of her hands from her bosom and wrung them together.

I said, "Mr. Patchett and I were discussing Mr. Jaspers's son by his first wife."

She cast a scared-horse glance at Patchett, whose mouth opened to protest, and another toward Bierce, who remained silent.

"Oh—but he wasn't William's! He was that other man's son! He was that Larrikin man's!"

She widened her eyes at Patchett as though he should throw her a life preserver.

"What do you mean, coming here and bullying this lady!" Patchett roared, when he had gotten his breath back.

Bierce spoke up suddenly. "I'm afraid I must bully her further. Mrs. Jaspers, I know your husband possessed a notebook taken from the Reverend Devine's study, containing names."

There was a silence so intense it could have been cut into blocks and installed in a library. Patchett moved closer to the desk, thus seeming to loom.

"If you please, Mrs. Jaspers," Bierce said. "In the interest of the investigation of your husband's death, I must have that little book."

Mrs. Jaspers tottered as though she might faint. In an instant Patchett was at her side, arm around her waist.

She whispered, "It is in the bottom right-hand drawer, Mr. Bierce. There is a false back."

I explored the drawer, found the false back and, in the space behind it, the little book. It had a brown leather cover. I handed it to Bierce, who pocketed it without opening it.

"Mrs. Jaspers, I assume this," he said. "Your husband discovered your indiscretion, and ordered you to steal this book, which he knew must exist. Is that correct?"

"Yes," she whispered, leaning on Patchett.

"Your husband made a small fortune from the names he found in the book. Were you aware of that?"

She stared at him, round-eyed. She shook her head slowly. She whispered, "No!" leaning on Frank Patchett, who said, "Haven't you troubled this lady enough, Mr. Bierce? Redmond? Please leave here now!"

Bierce said, "Mr. Patchett, if you are giving the orders in this household you will have told us something else that we are interested in knowing."

Patchett opened his mouth to speak, but thought better of it. Mrs. Jaspers had covered the lower part of her face with one of her white hands.

"Thank you for your cooperation, Mr. Patchett," Bierce said. "And yours, Mrs. Jaspers."

And we took our leave.

....

When we were out on steep Taylor Street I told Bierce, "He has moved into Jaspers's house and into his study, and, I'll bet, into his bed. That appears to be a Free Love lady of some accomplishments."

"And he is Jaspers's son," Bierce said. "Sayles's son with Milly Patchett."

We turned onto Pine Street. "He has not admitted it," I said.

"He may not unless he is forced to."

I said, "Clever to figure she had the little book."

"Jaspers had to have had it. Therefore, he must have forced her to obtain it. I doubt it will be of much use to us.

"Mrs. Jaspers could certainly be furnished with motives for murdering both her husband and her lover. But the requirement of 'Why now?' is by no means satisfied.

"I have spent much more time than I liked at the God Is Love Church," he went on. "I have interviewed the flower lady; the pianist; the choir lady; the sweeper lady, Mrs. Kurtz; and Deacon Robbins again. I wonder if you will see if we can dismiss Miss Mary Belcher from our calculations."

I said I would do so.

"She is employed as a typewriter at the *Chronicle*. I would rather attend the God Is Love Church than expose myself to that disreputable newspaper."

We walked on downtown. Bierce patted his pocket, where the book was.

....

The first person I encountered in the *Chronicle* Building was Jake Burgess, leaning on a counter as though he'd been waiting for me and smirking like a blond subordinate devil.

"Willie finally got wise to you, did he?"

"What do you mean?"

"Looking for a job here?"

I said I was looking for a typist named Mary Belcher.

"That old Devine suit, is it?" He patted a yawn. "Take you right to her."

Mary Belcher sat alone before a typewriter at a table in a big room surrounded by walls of reference books. She was a straight-backed young woman in a white shirtwaist with a great deal of dark brown hair stacked on her head so that the back of her neck was exposed.

"Company, girls!" Jake said, and she jumped.

He left us alone, however, and I made the acquaintance of the young woman who had sued the Reverend Devine for a breach of promise. She was plain-faced, with big eyes and a generous mouth that looked made for laughing, but she did not laugh when I broached my subject.

"How tiresome," she said. "I've been interviewed by so many people."

"This is the last one," I said.

She indicated a chair against one of the book walls. I seated myself and said, "Tell me something you've told no one else."

"There is nothing that I've told no one else."

"Is it possible to get you to smile while on this topic?"

"No!" she said, but she smiled.

"I've talked to several of Henry Devine's mistresses. An experience with him has been described as being enfolded in angel wings, as—"

"Please!" But her straight-backed stance relaxed a little. I was endeavoring to be charming.

"One person said he was not so beautiful on the inside as the outside."

She smiled again.

"He gave out pearls. Did he give you pearls?"

"Not enough for a necklace, Mr. Redmond."

"But he did offer marriage?"

"He did. His wife had just died and we couldn't be married for a year. The year passed. I suppose those magical words also worked for other stupid young women."

"Angel wings?"

She colored very prettily, the pink sweeping up from her throat to brighten her cheeks. She was more attractive than I had first thought.

"The fact is," she continued, "when the year had passed, I didn't really want to marry him. Yes, he *was* more beautiful on the outside. But I just didn't think he should be allowed to get out of his promise to me."

"Even though you didn't want to marry him."

"Even though I had come to the conclusion that he was a great fraud. Not even a fraud. That was just the way he'd been made by his Maker. Like a—like a—I don't know, like a very beautiful icing on a cake that is not much of a cake. The cake can't help what it is. You know, I almost became sorry for him for having nothing to offer, who seemed to offer so much."

I said, "I'm trying to find out if any one of his mistresses or the men in their lives killed him for his offerings, or the lack of them."

"My husband swore he would kill him. I told him it wasn't worth doing."

"Your husband?"

"I had a husband. I don't know if I have any more. He's gone off to Wisconsin to his mother, who understands him." For the first time she sounded bitter.

"Bad luck," I said.

"Just stupidity. Will women never learn about men?"

"Should I investigate your husband in Wisconsin?"

"I wouldn't bother. It was nice to hear him say he would kill Henry, once or twice. Then it seemed that whenever he thought about me that's what he thought about. It would take more of a man than John to shoot Henry Devine in the heart."

"John Belcher?"

"John Parkinson."

"The judge threw it out of court?"

"I had letters from Henry Devine in which he referred to me as his wife. But he had signed them 'Bunny' and the handwriting couldn't be proven to be his. By that time, as I said, I didn't care much. I thought it was good that I'd caused him a tolerable amount of unpleasantness and scandal, but after a while I couldn't even feel pleased about that. He was just a piece of pretty cake that wasn't much good and couldn't help it."

"Pearls again," I said. "On Devine's desk we found a little cup with two pearls in it. Do you have any idea what this might signify?"

"He loved pearls."

"There were a couple of dozen more in a cigar box in a drawer. I know that he presented pearls to ladies whose favors he had enjoyed. Could it be that pearls represented such interludes?"

She was silent for a time, her folded hands tented before her lips. She nodded.

"You see," I said, "there is a confusion here with the Trey of Pearls of the Suffrage movement. It is known that one of them had an affair with Devine. Does that account for the fact that there were two pearls instead of three? Did he then have his eye on the other two?"

"I think you need not concern yourself, Mr Redmond.

The pearls were in the cup on his desk because he loved pearls. He identified with pearls, as something having been formed into a perfect, glistening object from a flaw of the oyster. He considered himself a perfect glistening object, with an original flaw."

"Which was?"

"Womanizing."

"Thank you, Mrs. Parkinson," I said. "I wish I could assure you you'd never be bothered about this again."

"Thank you," she said, and returned to her typing table as I went out the door.

Jake was waiting for me in the hall.

"I suppose you'll be attending the Trey of Pearls' speaking at Falcon Hall tomorrow night, Tom."

"I'll be there. You?"

"Wouldn't miss it! There may be more ladies in the audience than they are counting on." He smirked at me.

"What's that mean?"

"You'll see."

I was unreasonably irritated by his rejoinder.

....

That evening, after I returned from the baths on Kearny Street pleasantly flushed and clean, I had not been in my rooms three minutes when a sharp knock sounded. When I opened the door Patchett followed inside a revolver held at chin level.

My first thought was that he was too large a man to have been the one outlined in the cone of light under the streetlight.

He backed against the door to close it, and lowered the revolver. He was very pale.

"There's a warrant out on me," he said. "Are you and Bierce responsible for that?"

I shook my head. "Probably Mr. Bank President Stevens."

"*Why,* man?"

I pointed to the chair by the door, and seated myself. Patchett sat down with his revolver still displayed in his lap.

"Some kind of financial misappropriations he thought he had discovered."

"I don't believe that!"

I shrugged.

He leaned forward. "Listen, Redmond, that old fart flails around at everybody. Mr. Jaspers saved that bank from going under. He was as honest a man as I ever met. I won't hear anything against William Jaspers!"

"You are probably going to have to," I said. "He was blackmailing a number of Devine's prayer-ladies from that little book Mrs. Jaspers light-fingered. It will probably all come out."

"Listen, Redmond—" he started, and forgot what he had planned to say.

"You picked up the money at least once that we know of," I said. "From Mr. Carling."

He opened his mouth and closed it.

Patchett had been victimized by his master.

"You'd better face some facts," I said. "The Grand Noble Humbug of E Clampus Vitas was a blackmailer, and maybe more than that."

"Why is there a warrant out for *me*?" he said weakly.

"You were his assistant and cashier."

Patchett was one sick assistant and cashier. "What should I do, Redmond?"

My reply produced itself without a thought, so that as I was saying her name I wondered why I had come up with it. "I'd get in touch with Mammy Pleasant."

"Why?"

"She may be interested in your case. She swings a heavy bat in the City."

He look puzzled, sweaty, and pale. "Well, maybe I will, then," he said in a voice he had probably meant to be arrogant. He rose. His revolver had disappeared into his pocket. He left.

I had the warm sensation of having done a good thing.

CHAPTER NINETEEN

RESPLENDENT, adj. Like a simple American citizen beduking himself in his lodge, or affirming his consequence in the Scheme of Things as an elemental unit of a parade.

—The Devil's Dictionary

TUESDAY, MARCH 2, 1892

Tuesday night was the grand pre-parade Suffragist meeting at Falcon Hall. Bierce had decided that he would attend with me. He was in a sour mood when we partook of whiskey at Blessington's before the meeting.

Mrs. Atherton had resigned from the *Examiner* and left San Francisco.

"The Ella Wheeler Wilcox letters were the last straw," he said. "She wishes to be a novelist again. She's taken rooms at Fort Ross, up the coast. I am to assist her with her novel by mail. The title is *The Doomswoman.*"

"She took your advice as to a title."

"I admire her, but there is a certain promise in the flesh that does not obtain in the post."

And after a while he said, "I believe she was more interested in Sam anyway. It is curious that he is the newspaper's editor but I am *her* editor."

It was a foggy night as we made our way down Market

Street toward Falcon Hall. The gas lights and arc lights made misty balls of illumination. A heavy traffic of horse cars and drays clattered over the paving stones, hacks and buggies heading toward the ferries. Lights glared out of the fog from the saloons and showplaces we passed, in the wake of a pair of prostitutes rapping along in their boots, waggling their hips and casting smiles over their shoulders at us.

A good crowd was assembling at Falcon Hall. A number of derby-hatted men clotted around the entry as women, many in Suffragist white gowns, filed inside past them. The hall was a cavernous space with a shrilling of female conversation; hundreds of women, some seated, some standing, many in white dresses and yellow ribbons to show loyalty to their cause. Some men clustered together, but not many. On the stage was a lectern covered with a red cloth, and decorated with the yellow ribbons. With whiffs of perfume and perspiration and a great bustle of converse the women settled themselves into an audience, while Bierce and I seated ourselves on the aisle, where we were subject to unfriendly glances. On the other side of the main body of seats I saw Jake Burgess and the *Chronicle* columnist Marshall McGee.

Bierce was still thinking about Mrs. Atherton. "A beautiful woman," he said. "But a prickly personality. Women are the opposite of the cactus plant, smooth and comely on the outside but a mess of snakes and needles on the inside."

I thought he would be neatening that up for inclusion in "Prattle." It reminded me of Amanda speaking of her lover the Reverend Devine.

When the audience had settled, with a patrolman stationed at each exit, Mrs. Quinan—wearing white with yellow ribbons—presented herself, spoke a few words, and introduced Emmiline Prout. Emmiline was handsome and rather dashing, with her black eyes and crown of black hair. She repeated the speech on suffragism I had heard from her before, and she made a good impression. The audience seemed to me very quiet, with no objections from the males present over her words, and a prolonged applause when she had finished.

Gloria Robinson appeared as Emmy disappeared, approaching the lectern at her slouching gait, clad in the same pristine white with a kind of boa of yellow ribbons. Bird Girl did her bird calls to appreciative applause, and promised to sing later in the program. And then it was Amanda's turn.

What an attractive presence she was, with her quick-stepping gait, her white garb and yellow ribbons, her vivid face with the lock of fair hair curved across her forehead. The applause for her was prolonged. Finally, hands raised for silence, she said: "I come to speak to you against marriage, the body and soul destroying institution of the Christian Church and the American state!"

My heart sank. There was a kind of universal intake of breath at her words, and she stood in silence for a long moment, straight-backed and high-headed at the lectern, her right fist pressed mortar and pestle into the left palm.

Beside me Bierce was stirring in irritation. He must detest this place, full of women, and he was surely troubled by Amanda's opinions, which were so close to his own.

She continued: "I come to speak to you in favor of Free Love, which is honest, responsible, and open sexual encounter between two equal partners. However, Free Love is impossible if the partners are married. Equality is surely not possible if one of the partners is a slave. Freedom and love are therefore the enemies of marriage."

Between her statements she waited so long that I became

uncomfortable, and the silence throughout the audience seemed to me to bode ill. I heard Bierce clucking his tongue.

"Your cousin is a very effective speaker," he whispered to me.

Amanda continued: "Marriage is comparable to prostitution because in either case the female provides access to her body in return for economic support—The Material Necessity."

Here she took two steps to her right, and then two steps back. With a slow motion she jammed her fist into her left palm again.

"In Christian marriage as we know it the woman owes sexual obedience to her husband. She is his slave. She does not own herself, he does. Marriage is a license for rape, and that rape can be daily and nightly, as often as the slavemaster requires it."

Bierce was clucking quietly again.

As Amanda continued in her firm, sweet voice, I saw my hopes for love and marriage and a child to satisfy my mother pass glimmering out the window.

Presently she changed the subject.

"I have heard it said that the Suffragist and Free Love movements are the creatures of the Women's Christian Temperance Union, and the Anti-saloon League.

"Let me tell you of women's bias against the saloon: It is both a symbol and a weapon of male supremacy. Alcohol not only lessens self-control, it stimulates lust. With his lust stimulated in the exclusively male preserve of the saloon, the husband comes home and rapes his wife.

"If she divorces him for a life of rape and physical abuse she loses livelihood and children. For two thousand years Christianity has preached Jesus and practiced Moses. The errant female is stoned, the errant male goes free.

"Let me read to you from correspondence from unfortunate women that has been addressed to me." She plucked a folded piece of paper from the lectern, and read: "I was a girl of sixteen, full of life and health when I became a wife and a slave in every sense of the word. Never was I free from my husband's brutal outrages, morning, noon, and night. Often this torture would last an hour or two. One night it lasted four hours!"

A triumphant whistle sounded from the other side of the hall, followed hard by a storm of indignant hushes. Amanda waited at the lectern, unsmiling.

"Another," she said.

"This young man whom I had thought to love, and had married, threatened me with a sharp knife because I had refused to perform on him an oral office disgusting to me, which he insisted upon."

There was another vast whisper of breath intakes.

"Another," Amanda said. She read from a third letter: "I am nearly wrecked and ruined by nightly intercourse, which is often repeated in the morning. This and nothing else was the cause of my miscarriage. My husband went to work on me like a man a-mowing.

"Another," she said.

"I was married when I was sixteen, my husband twenty-two. He called me unaccommodating and capricious, and if I refused him his strong fingers would grasp my flesh and force me to submission. He gave me a good home, I did not have to work, no doubt he did not intend to be unreasonable, but he said, 'You are my wife and the sooner you do as I say the sooner we will have peace.' I would resolve not to resist again, but my Scotch blood and instinct for freedom were too strong. As a result I was bruised and beaten. Two little babies were literally killed before they were born, and the one who did live fell so often into convulsions when he should have been safe in the womb that when at last I watched his little flame go out, I knew he was spared a life of imbecility and idiocy, and I could not mourn—"

A file of large Negresses burst through the far door, past the patrolman there. They wore white dresses, with Suffragist yellow ribbons fluttering. There was a chorus of protest. The black women began posturing and uttering bird calls, mainly rooster crowing. They advanced down the aisle toward the stage.

They were men in blackface and dresses; this was an invasion of E Clampus Vitas.

They trooped up onto the dais, where Amanda stood her ground. They grouped around her and I found myself on my feet.

"They will not dare to harm her!" Bierce said, his hand on my arm.

They began to sing "The Battle Hymn of the Republic," off key and off the beat, stamping their boots in time to their ragged singing, the cock-a-doodle man emitting his rooster calls at intervals. The women in the audience were standing, shouting at them, waving arms, waving umbrellas. The two policemen forced their way to the foot of the stage. I made my way down the aisle through the gesticulating women, and vaulted onto the dais. Two men were manhandling Amanda; I saw they were trying to raise her to their shoulders.

"Unhand her!" I said, grasping one of them by the shoulder. Amanda's terrified face jerked toward me and black faces regarded me, all of them with mouths open, roaring the words to Bird Girl's hymn, with the rooster call punctuating. The two released Amanda to me.

They all looked as though they were having a fine time.

I shook off a friendly arm, and, holding Amanda, banged our way out of their midst. Further back on the stage I could see Emmy and Bird Girl crouched on either side of Mrs. Quinan.

I got Amanda off the stage without interference because the merry Clampers had busied themselves helping the two policemen onto the dais to include them in their choir, their singing now drowned by the outcry from the standing women.

"Take me away from here, Tom!" Amanda whispered to me. Arms around her, I rammed the two of us through the crowding women and outside into the cool fog and misty lights of Market Street. I flagged down a hackie and directed him to Sacramento Street, with Amanda shivering against me.

....

In my rooms I poured brandy. Amanda slumped silently on the settee, sipping, from time to time emitting sighs of recovery.

"I was so frightened!" she said finally. "But I don't think they meant any real harm."

"They meant to make you look ridiculous."

"By making themselves ridiculous?"

"That's what they do." I was trying to think if I had seen Frank Patchett's face among those black faces.

She put down her brandy hardly touched and folded her hands together in her lap, gazing down at them. When she looked up at me again her face was still white as milk.

"I'm so tired of being a fraud," she said in a small voice.

"Stop being one."

"Would you give me a divorce if I wasn't happy?"

It was a moment before I understood the reference. My heart leaped in my chest. "I'll put it in writing," I said.

"And if we had children, that I could take them if I wanted, if we divorced?"

"That too."

"I do trust you, I think."

"Well, I love you, I think."

"May I spend the night?" she asked, looking down again.

"If I have your promise."

"Maybe!" she said

I plumped myself down beside my cousin Amanda to embrace her and kiss her damp, loved face.

CHAPTER TWENTY

PANTOMIME, n. A play in which the story is told without violence to the language. The least disagreeable form of dramatic action.
—The Devil's Dictionary

WEDNESDAY, MARCH 3, 1892

In the morning, the morning of the parade, a crisp, bright late-winter morning, Mammy Pleasant was in Bierce's office when I looked in. He motioned me to a seat.

Mammy's dark face peered at me out of the hood of her bonnet. "You told that young man to look me up."

"I did, Mrs. Pleasant."

"They are trying to blame that young man for mischief of William Jaspers at the bank!"

I was pleased that I had guessed correctly. Patchett was the son of an octoroon mother, although his complexion was no darker than mine, and I didn't think his blood much different. But the essential distinction was important to Mammy Pleasant.

"Bring me what information you have and I will see what I can do with it," Bierce said, meaning a piece in "Prattle."

"I will do that, Mr. Bierce," Mammy said, and added, "I believe Mrs. Jaspers will stick by him."

"That is interesting."

"I have put it to Mr. Bosworth Curtis to defend him."

"That will certainly be a help, Mrs. Pleasant," Bierce said.

When she had departed, he said to me, "She is fierce for her race, and that is as it should be."

I said, "A shock to Patchett to discover his sainted pa the banker was a thief as well as a blackmailer."

Bierce had brought a wad of newsprint out of a desk drawer and unfolded it. He flourished the *Sacramento Bee* my father had sent me, which I, bored with Sacramento brag, had not perused.

"Regard this!" he said, slapping the newspaper down beside the skull.

It was the gushy article about the wonders of the Beal estate in Sacramento. "The marked paragraph," Bierce said.

"—and wonder of wonders, a huge room in the attic. The *Marche aux Oiseaux*, as it is called in French, Mrs. Beal's native tongue, is an aviary of mechanical birds, perfectly formed little creatures at rest on the limbs of a spreading tree that somehow was introduced into this grand room. At the push of a button these charming little fellows burst into song, each with his distinctive bird call. Their heads raised, tiny throats on the strain, their notes from nature float out into this room of wonders . . ."

"The *Marche aux Oiseaux,*" Bierce said. "The marching *osos,* the marching bears.

"When those Clampers dressed in female garments burst into the hall last evening with their bird calls, the thought of transvestism came to me. Now it is confirmed. *Oiseaux. Osos.* And Gloria Robinson, who was Robert Morton, their attendant."

It was Bird Girl who had taken a shot at me, Bird Girl who—

"I have notified Captain Chandler," Bierce said. "Who has sent to arrest him—*her*!"

"Let's go there!" I said.

....

All was confusion at the Cyrus Hotel; we found two patrolmen and a detective in the suite with Amanda, Emmy, and Mrs. Quinan. Mrs. Quinan was seated on a settee alone, staring out the window, while the others shouted at each other. Amanda's tear-stained face was frantic.

"Ran for it and locked herself in her room," the detective explained to Bierce. "Then she got out someway, over the transom maybe. Anyhow, she has made off."

Patrolman Peterson was red-faced with embarrassment, Emmy jabbering at him. Amanda came to me. "How did you *know*?"

I told her about the bird calls.

"I found the gold eagles he had taken from Henry's pockets," she said. "I told him I knew he was the one. I told him he must go to Mr. Bierce. He thinks I betrayed him. He says he will kill me!"

"You didn't betray him."

"He's got a gun!"

"Says he's got a gun!" the other patrolman was saying.

"Armed and dangerous!" the detective said.

"I suppose the parade is off," I said.

Mrs. Quinan heard me, and rose from her seat and turned to me. "It is not off, sir! We will proceed!" She came toward us, a big woman, very regal. "Amanda, I simply can't believe this of you. You knew she was a boy, you played your shameful games with him. And he has murdered two men, one out of simple jealousy for your favors!"

"Free Love was the game we played," Amanda said in a strained voice. "You gave it lip service also, Mrs. Q."

"I am simply furious. What a blow you have dealt us!"

Amanda stared into my face, blinking back tears. Her lips mouthed the words, "Do you hate me?"

"Quite the opposite," I said.

"We will have our parade!" Mrs. Quinan said in a carrying voice. "The remaining two of the Trey will ride with me on the float. How will we safeguard Miss Wilson, you policemen?"

....

So it was decided that I would take Bird Girl's place on the float. I struggled into one of Mrs. Quinan's white dresses, which was narrow in the shoulders, generous in the bust, so small in the waist it could hardly be laced at the back, and voluminous in the skirt. I was presented with a number of yellow ribbons, a cloche hat loaded with silk flowers, and a shawl to cover my big feet in their male boots that could not be otherwise concealed. I was given a police revolver, secreted in a velvet bag, to protect Amanda from Bird Girl.

The accumulation of my female disguise much amused Ambrose Bierce, who promised to walk nearby with his own weapon. The start of the parade was at Market and Eighth, where no doubt a host of Suffragist sympathizers, among them Mrs. George Hearst, would join us. Somewhere farther east on Market the black-faced Clampers would perform whatever tricks and humiliations they had planned, involving trumpets and horns, as Bierce had suggested. A brigade of policemen all along the route would be on the lookout for Robert Morton, the murderer and transvestite.

Milling at the corner of Eighth and Market on this sunny, cool, and breezy morning were hundreds of ladies in white dress and yellow ribbons that blew about gracefully in the currents of air. The float was there; two mules stood in their mulish dejection with no gender to celebrate hitched to a flat platform bearing a kind of throne for Mrs. Quinan. A round-shouldered colored man in overalls and an old hat that had been doffed and donned too many times sat hunched behind the mules, his whip slanting over them like a fishing pole from a creek bank.

I was to lounge more or less at Mrs. Q.'s feet, the shawl covering my own unfemale boots. Emmy and Amanda were to position theselves at the front corners of the platform, each with a basket of blooms for the scattering of flowers. White-clad female sergeants were forming the supporting ladies into ranks. Amanda, white-faced, surveyed the men and women who lined the curbs on either side. Emmiline drank from a pitcher of water the two of them shared. With good reason, she did not look as frightened as Amanda.

My legs were chilly in my dress until I learned how to drape it around them, and my hat had to be constantly adjusted. Above me, Mrs. Quinan radiated authority over the whole affair without having to lift her voice. I suppose she made some signal to start us off.

The mules strained in their harness to get the float moving. Behind us, amid cries of command, the ladies lined up with their arms linked and half-filled Market Street, four ranks of them stepping briskly along in their Suffragist white dresses, behind them a moving congregation of more women not wearing white but displaying the yellow ribbons of the cause.

In my tensely lounging position I felt a part of something very large and very potent. The sound of Market Street was not now the vast rumble of wheels on cobbles, but of marching female sharp-heeled boots. Above me I could hear Mrs. Q. muttering, perhaps praying. Amanda and

Emmy flung their flowers gracefully-graciously to either side. With what I hoped was Bird Girl pretense and some dignity I made an arm-raised gesture saluting something or other. So we progressed along the great thoroughfare, our eyes searching the faces on either side, headed toward the gray slice of Bay at the end of Market Street.

The mules pulled more easily with the momentum of the rolling float as we passed buildings bearing signs: PRINGLE BROS. FINE SHOES; DR. THOMAS L. HILL, DENTEST; J. PORCHER, IMPORTER OF HATS AND CAPES; G. BERSON, CARPETS, FURNITURE, ETC. As we approached Seventh Street, I searched for Bird Girl/Robert Morton in the crowds of men and women lining the street. Men whistled; some booed, the women with them cheering and calling out. A group of fellows gathered outside Hansen's Saloon made rude gestures. We rolled past four- and five-story buildings with empty windows, signs advertizing EAGLE PRINTING, RUBBER STAMPS, CARPET AND FURNITURE WAREHOUSE, OVERLAND TICKET OFFICE, ELCHO HOUSE, LIQUORS, and the block long mass of THE EMPORIUM.

Amanda and Emmy flung their flowers, the two beautiful Pearls leading the way for the ranks of the not-so-beautiful Suffragists with their linked arms forming lines of sisterhood. I tried to pretend that I was a pretty Suffragist, maybe a Free Lover, even a varietist, as I waved to the acclaim and disparagement of the male and female crowds along the sidewalk. Above me, Mrs. Q. muttered her prayers or incantations.

We approached Fourth Street, the mules plodding headjerking along, the young women flinging flowers. We passed more signs: MARTIN SONS CLOAK AND SUIT HOUSE, OYSTER ROLLS, CONGREVE'S SALLON, THE KNICKERBOCKER, LIQUORS, BLESSINGTON'S, THE PUNCH, WINES AND LIQUORS.

The plan was this: If Amanda spotted Robert Morton/

Bird Girl or any danger, she was to flee back to my protection. Two policemen marched on either side of the float, and Bierce must be out there somewhere. Behind us the Suffragists stepped along in spritely fashion. Along the way now were the baseball Firemen, who didn't recognize me, printers with inky aprons, and messenger boys from the *Examiner*. My teammates were armed with baseball bats and looked ready for action.

We approached Cape Horn, where Third Street emptied into Market from the south, and Kearny and Geary converged to the north. Faces watched from every window here. Along the south side was a concentration of saloons; here was where we expected the Clampers' attack.

Mrs. Quinan uttered a groan as though she'd been struck. A gang of men streamed out of the south-side saloons, not five hundred of them, but twenty or thirty, all the sturdy young drinkingmen that the Clamper who had replaced Jaspers could muster. The tremendous and discordant blast of trumpets had the effect of halting the mules in their tracks. Clampers were blowing a variety of horns; others were beating on dishpans, pan lids, and kerosene tins with sticks.

The blare of the horns faded, and I saw that the corps of *Examiner* messenger boys had confronted the hornsmen sucking on lemons, which effectively stifled the trumpeting Clampers in their own saliva. One of the boys clambered onto the float to mime the lemon sucking broadly, until Mrs. Quinan hissed him away. The horns soured off, all but silenced, but the beating on metal increased. The drumming Clampers came on in their white dresses.

I leaped to my feet, stripping off my hat. "FIREMEN!"

They answered the summons, rushing—bats raised—

toward the float, pitifully few of them engaging the Clampers, but reenforced directly by the *Examiner* forces.

The metallic banging increased in volume to become unbearable, in a powerful outcry both male and female from all around. The ranks of Suffragists closed around the float. Emmy and Amanda still stood at their fore corners but no longer tossed petals.

Some of the Clampers wore blackface and their white gowns from the previous evening, and these came in force up against the south side of the float, where Amanda was. She retreated from them as I stood before Mrs. Quinan, hat off, with my velvet bag in my hand.

Mrs. Quinan screamed *"Gloria!"*

I saw him; he was one of them, in his white dress, a slender figure, a feminine but not feminine face, queer eyes slitted with madness. I saw the glint of metal in his raised hand. Forgetting my own weapon, I flung myself upon him from the float. The report of his revolver deafened me.

I sprawled on the paving stones on top of Bird Girl, twisting the revolver from his grasp and slamming him on the chin with it. Rising and kneeling over him, I could see one white-clad figure lying on the float on her back, shot, and another bending over her.

I clouted Bird Girl in fury again, all around us shouts and screaming. Bierce had a grip on my arm, saying "Tom . . . Tom . . . She is unharmed!" holding me off from killing Robert Morton.

CHAPTER TWENTY-ONE

INFANCY, n. The period of our lives when, according to Wordsworth, "Heaven lies about us." The world begins lying about us pretty soon afterward.

— *The Devil's Dictionary*

WEDNESDAY, MARCH 3, 1892

It was not Amanda crying noisily, supine on the float, it was Emmiline, with a splash of blood on the shoulder of her dress. Amanda was trying to stanch the wound with her scarf. A plug-hatted doctor with his hardshell bag climbed up the north side of the float, calling out, "Let me attend to that!"

Behind me two police had Bird Girl on his feet, with his mat of brown hair standing up in disarray around his bloody face. Alongside the float—in silence now—the black-faced Clampers stood, staring at what they must be afraid they had wrought. Amanda flung herself into my arms.

"He's killed Emmy!"

"She's not killed," I said, and the doctor looked up and made a reassuring motion with his hand. Emmy's sobs were punctuated with squeals of pain. Mrs. Quinan sat on her throne with her hands framing her strained face. The black-face Clampers drifted back away from the stalled float.

In the heavy silence, they retreated to their saloons. Bird

Girl was hustled away by the two policemen. The doctor and another man assisted Emmiline off the float. Mrs. Quinan rose to regard her ranks of Suffragists, who were standing behind the float in anxious disarray. She made a commanding gesture. She declaimed in a harsh voice:

They never fall who gravely plead for right,
God's faithful martyrs can not suffer loss.
Their blazing faggots sow the world with light
Heaven's gate swings open on their bloody cross!

"Come with me!" I said to Amanda.

"We are going on!" she said, detaching herself.

"I'm not!" I fluffed out the sides of my dress, which I now detested.

She faced me hard-faced for a moment, before she bent to her basket and picked up a handful of blossoms.

"Proceed!" Mrs. Quinan called out, standing and waving an arm forward like a cavalry commander. Behind us, Suffragists scurried to reform their lines.

The colored driver flicked his whip over the backs of the mules. The float groaned as it began to move. Amanda stood smiling out at the spectators who lined the sidewalks, scattering her blossoms with graceful gestures, the last of the Trey of Pearls.

I stood watching the platform roll slowly away down Market Street, moving aside so as not to block the first rank of marching women in white, with their breeze-fluttered ribbons.

Bierce came to join me as I was jerking at my dress, which was too tight across the shoulders.

"I believe they will have their way as to their suffrage," he said sourly.

....

In Willie Hearst's office I discovered that Sam Chamberlain had organized the lemon-sucking boys who had trumped the trumpeters. He was very pleased with himself.

"George Atherton himself could not have made a better job of it!"

"Has Mrs. Hearst expressed an opinion about the parade?" I asked Willie.

"She was shocked at the horn-blowing and the shooting," he said. "But she was most impressed that Mrs. Quinan caused the parade to continue."

Bierce explained to Willie Hearst and Sam Chamberlain what had happened. I did not mind his taking the credit for discovering the identity of Robert Morton, who must be Mme. Starr's jack of hearts, and I, who had clubbed him into insensibility, the black jack.

"It seems that Robert Morton had had some experience in Colfax portraying a female in school entertainments," Bierce said. "There is no knowing why he decided to pose as a female when he left his employment at the Beal estate, but it is probable that he identified with the feminist cause because of the miseries his mother had suffered, and no doubt it was easier to become a feminist if one became a female."

"He has not said much," I put in. "He has a broken jaw and a concussion and is heavily bandaged."

"He took some belaboring from Tom," Bierce said.

Willie gazed at me, frowning as though we were relating ordinary matters of a world he could hardly imagine. His direct gaze was disconcerting because his blade of a nose made him look cross-eyed. Sam lounged in his chair.

"Gee whiz!" he said, and chuckled.

"Some of this information is privileged because of Tom's

relation to his cousin, Miss Wilson," Bierce went on. "The theory is this: Morton, in female dress and with his hair grown long, took up with the Suffragist group led by Mrs. Quinan in Denver. Miss Wilson discovered his true gender but none of the others did. Miss Wilson engaged in a relation with him. I will point out here that Miss Wilson is a declared follower of the doctrine of Free Love."

I thought she had embraced it to rationalize her trysts with Robert Morton, even though she had told me they had ventured no further than she and I had. But she had ventured further with the Reverend Devine. I could understand Robert Morton's jealousy.

Willie looked shocked.

Bierce continued: "Here in San Francisco Miss Wilson entered into an affair with the Reverend Devine, who was, of course, a notorious seducer of his parishioners. Robert Morton, inflamed with jealousy, shot him."

"That is very clever, Mr. Bierce," Willie said.

"And then Tom Redmond's story was printed concerning William Jaspers and his first wife, who was Robert Morton's mother," Sam said. He was very spruce this morning, hair carefully brushed, monocle hanging on its black cord, a blossom in his buttonhole. Not one of Amanda's, I thought.

"Robert Morton must have thought it a remarkable coincidence," Bierce said. "His beloved mother had lived and died in misery because of William Jaspers, and must have filled her son with a bushel basket of the wrongs done her. And here he was, already a murderer, with his mother's persecutor identified and close at hand. So Robert Morton, who had managed to conceal his identity within the skirts of Gloria Robinson, killed Jaspers."

"There is much still to be checked," Sam said, twirling his monocle on its cord.

"I think we can proceed," Willie said. "Will you and Mr. Redmond begin the writing, Mr. Bierce?"

"We will do so," Bierce said.

"It would be very timely if young Morton would corroborate some of this."

I said, "Captain Chandler says that if he does not wish to give us the information we require, he has the means of inducing cooperation."

"I am sure he does," Sam said, laughing. "Tell me, Ambrose, what has become of the assistant to Jaspers you suspected for a time?"

"He is in police custody. Old Garrett Stevens of the Cumberland Bank has filed charges against him and Jaspers for misappropriation of funds. Young Patchett is most probably the son of Jaspers and a St. Louis octoroon named Milly Patchett. He has retained the cleverest lawyer in town, Bosworth Curtis, through the good offices of Mammy Pleasant, who is always concerned with the welfare of people of her race."

"Tell us how you solved these puzzles, Ambrose."

It was the part Bierce liked best, I knew, and indeed he deserved the credit. I had not made the connection with the female-clad Clampers and Bird Girl. Furthermore, I had chosen to disregard the description of Governor Beal's mansion from the *Sacramento Bee*, considering it only another piece of my father's Sacramento boostering.

Of course I would have understood also, had I read the piece.

Bierce went over it all in some detail. I nodded with an approbation I did not entirely feel. I couldn't get Amanda out of my mind, slim and graceful, proud and courageous in white, alone on the front of the Suffragist float, tossing out blossoms with what had appeared to be a sincere smile.

"Tell me, Mr. Redmond," Willie said. "What can Miss Wilson object to here? She is a professed Free Lover."

A varietist also.

I said, "As I have heard Ambrose Bierce explain quite a few times now, a specific is much more powerful than a generalization."

"I am not certain that I understand that."

"Free Love is a generalization. Actual sexual relations with two different men is specific."

"Yes, I see."

"I believe Bierce and I can euphemize it," I said. "I would like to try to do so."

"Euphemisms are less powerful than bare facts," Sam said.

"Let us to work, Tom," Bierce said. "When God made a tree he did not have to write about his accomplishment afterward. But journalists must."

At this even Willie Hearst grinned.

....

That evening Amanda came to see me in my rooms.

She wore a plain black frock with a black scoop bonnet, in which her pretty face looked small and wan. She embraced me, but with some reserve, I thought.

"How is Emmy?"

"Her shoulder was merely nicked. There was a lot of blood, but not much damage. You got to him in time, you see. You have everyone's thanks."

I nodded an everyone-is-welcome.

"What will they do to Robert?" she wanted to know.

"They will hang him."

She flinched.

"You discovered his cache of Devine's gold eagles," I said.

She nodded.

"Were you in love with him?" I demanded.

"It was only like puppies cuddling together!" Her eyes had filled and would not meet my eyes.

"What is the bad news you have brought me?" I said.

She moved forward and back with that motion familiar to me from watching her performance as speaker.

"You see, the British Suffrage Society has been urging Mrs. Quinan, and us, to come and help them because we have been effective. And we have planned to go there. We have promised."

"I know you have."

"Well, you see, Bobby's in jail and Emmy doesn't want to go on. So there is no one to go with Mrs. Quinan but me."

Tears gleamed in her eyes, which saved something of the moment.

"Cuz, I can't not!" she cried.

"Why not?"

"It's her *life*!"

"Is her life more important than ours?"

"It is all she has!"

In the ninth inning, down by one, the third out in progress and inevitable.

I regretted immediately saying, "Free Love has been a disaster for your partners, one dead and the other one to hang. Who else was favored?"

She gave me a long glance as though trying to forgive me. "No one of any importance except you," she said.

"Well, I love you," I said.

"I love you, too!"

"What will happen to us?"

"Cuz, I will go to England for a while, maybe three

months, maybe six months, and then I'll come back and say maybe again!"

It was lovely to think so.

"We'll write letters! Beautiful love letters!"

I would do that.

"I can spend the night!" she said. "Can we go out to dinner at one of the nice places you know, and then come back here and open a bottle of bubbly? You may kiss my bosom, if you like, my dearest Cuz!"

We could do that.

AFTERWORD

USAGE, n. The First Person of the literary Trinity, the Second and Third being Custom and Conventionality. Imbued with a decent reverence for the Holy Triad an industrious writer may hope to produce books that will live as long as the fashion.

—The Devil's Dictionary

Robert Morton corroborated almost exactly the narrative of Bierce's speculations. Amanda Wilson was not brought into the trial by name, but rather as an unidentified young woman. Bird Girl was convicted and sentenced to hang, but he died in the typhoid epidemic that swept through San Quentin Prison in 1893.

....

The Reverend George Stottlemyer was convicted of embezzlement and sentenced to the state penitentiary.

....

With Robert Morton dead and Frank Patchett indicted, Jaspers's paternities became moot. Patchett followed in Jaspers's footsteps, at least insofar as Mrs. Jaspers was concerned. Bosworth Curtis got him acquitted of the Cumberland Bank's charges, but the Bank then proceeded against Jaspers's estate. Patchett and Mrs. Jaspers cashed in her accounts and portable property, and disappeared from California in 1894.

Mrs. Jaspers and Frank Patchett had at least found True Love.

....

My correspondence with my own True Love flourished for a while, with protestations of love and promises of returns, but there was a perhaps-inevitable slackening. After a year, letters did not fly back and forth so frequently, and there was no more mention of a return.

She was, however, a grand success in England, where the public was unfamiliar with female speakers. I did gather that she had modified her rhetoric and was less the Free Lover and more the Suffragist. Indeed, the doctrine of Free Love had fallen out of favor with the Suffragists, and had become associated with the Anarchist Movement.

The news of her nuptials came over the wire service from New York in 1894—the marriage of the American Suffragist Speaker Miss Amanda Wilson to the Earl of Wessex, a nobleman of high rank, prominent in the support of the Women's Suffrage Movement in the United Kingdom.

The American girl of no fortune had won her British prince.

I received one last letter from my cousin: Her husband, Hubert, was older, a very sweet man, funny and crotchety, and she loved him very much. She hoped to bear a child.

"I always told you I was a terrible fraud," she wrote.

My heart was broken for a while, but recovered as time went by.

....

Bierce and Mrs. Atherton carried on a long correspondence, which on his part was her education in prose style. Her handwriting was so illegible that he confessed to me that he broke into a sweat whenever one of the multitudinous letters from Fort Ross arrived. Her letters are still extant, while his to her were destroyed in the 1906 Earthquake and Fire. No doubt a textbook on style was destroyed with them, but Bierce did publish a text on American usage, *Write It Right*, a paperback with a yellow cover that for years was carried in the pocket of every San Francisco newspaperman.

Mrs. Atherton wrote a novel, *A Christmas Witch*, with Bierce as the principal character, published in *Godey's* magazine. Bierce, named Arbuthnot in the novel, has withdrawn to a mountain refuge in his disgust at mankind, where his pleasures are books, solitude, and the woman Heloise, who is a spoiled, willful, and adventurous idealization of Gertrude Atherton. Arbuthnot indicates that he might be willing to fall in love with her when she matures.

Bierce was not pleased with his depiction and asked that the novel not be republished in book form, as was Mrs. Atherton's usual practice. She acceded to his wishes. However, he highly praised her Fort Ross novel, *The Doomswoman*. "In its class the book is superior to any that any Californian has done. It is luminous, full of color and movement, and resounding, if not with genius, with far more than the drone of a mere 'artist.' " Extravagant praise from Bierce for a novel!

For her part, Gertrude Atherton worried about Bierce's fame and the lack of it. After Fort Ross she returned to New York, where Bierce's name did not resound with genius. "I suppose I am more ambitious for you than for myself," she wrote him. "Publish in the East! Then you get circulation on both sides of the continent. Publish in the West and you do not get east of Pittsburgh."

In 1895 William Randolph Hearst purchased the *New York Journal* with a loan from his mother and moved much of the staff of the *Examiner*, including Bierce, to New York, to drum up a war with Spain over Cuba as a circulation enhancer. There Gertrude Atherton carried on something of an affair with Sam Chamberlain, abandoning him finally because of his hard drinking. She lived a peripatetic life, writing Bierce from Munich that "your picture hangs in my salon."

Bierce quarreled in time with most of his friends. He did not quarrel with Gertrude Atherton, but lost interest in her because of her indefatigible self-promotion. He had always feared she would become more illustrious than he, and she was certainly more notorious than "the wickedest man in San Francisco," whose fame had never traveled much further east than Pittsburgh.

She became a grand dame of American as well as Californian literature, and returned at last in some glory to finish out her years in San Francisco, where she received a Doctorate in Literature from Mills College, an honorary law degree from the University of California, and was guest of honor at "Gertrude Atherton Day" at the 1939 Golden Gate Exposition, where she was celebrated as "California's most famous daughter."

She failed, however, to be elected to the prestigious American Academy of Arts and Letters, which had honored the other living American female novelists, Ellen Glasgow and Willa Cather. She died in San Francisco in 1948, having published fifty-six works of fiction, nonfiction, and memoir.

....

And the Suffragists marched and spoke, argued and fulminated and pled, and gained inch by inch. On the wall of the

National American Women's Suffrage headquarters hung a map titled "Map of Woman Suffrage in the United States." At first there was on it only a single square of white marked "Wyoming 1869." In time, another square was added: "Colorado 1893." Then "Utah 1895," and "Idaho 1896." California was long stalled by the power of the liquor interests, especially in the Bay counties of San Francisco and Alameda, which had large populations of wine- and beer-drinking European immigrants, but finally "California 1912" joined the Map of Suffrage, along with Oregon and Arizona. The Western states were far ahead of the Eastern ones.

....

In 1915 the greatest of all the women's suffrage demonstrations was staged in New York City. The women marched in superb order, banners waving, bands playing, battalions of housewives, stenographers, typists, shopgirls, shirtwaist factory girls, nurses, troops of college graduates, five thousand schoolteachers, squads of society women—even Lillian Russell, "the toast of Broadway," who was usually transported in hansom cabs and limousines.

Fifty thousand women marched that day.

Along the sidewalks, watching women cheered and clapped until their hands ached, and hordes of male spectators cheerfully booed. Then came the vision, Miss Inez Milholland, the so-called "beauty of the suffrage movement," in sparkling white with yellow ribbons blowing, astride a tall white horse. It was said of her that this presence was as lovely and impressive as a square rigger under a full head of sail.

The male boos turned to cheers.

It was not long before the Nineteenth Amendment to the Constitution was passed.

By 1918 fourteen states had ratified, of the thirty-six

necessary. In the spring of 1920 it all came down to Tennessee, where the legislative chamber was filled with roses—yellow for suffrage, red for anti. One more vote for passage was lacking. Harry Burn, the youngest man in the legislature, had entered the chamber with a red rose in his buttonhole, but also with a note from his mother in his pocket, advising him to "be a good boy."

He voted "aye" and the Suffragists in the balcony burst into cheers. The Ninteenth Amendment had been ratified!

Women were enfranchised nationally in 1920, seventy-two years after their first convocation on their rights at Seneca Falls, and they were able to help elect to the White House that year the handsome philanderer Warren G. Harding.